# The Perfect Union

## Trina Lane

Published by Trina Lane

All Trademarks are the property of their respective owners

The Perfect Union

Cover Art by Angela Haddon

Digtial ISBN: 978-1-967648-03-0

Paperback ISBN: 978-1-967648-06-1

# Author's Note

♥

The original publication of this series spanned the years from 2010 to 2017. Although The Perfect Union was published as the first book in the series, it is actually the second book in terms of the timeline of events. With the release of the second editions of the series, I wanted to take this opportunity to reorder the books to accurately reflect their chronological order and ensure a more coherent reading experience for all my readers. While each book in the series functions as a self-contained narrative, allowing readers to enjoy them individually, I highly recommend reading the series sequentially to fully appreciate the character development and the evolving dynamics of their interconnected relationships, thus enhancing the overall reading experience. The books have all been enhanced with extra material that builds upon the foundation of their initial releases, resulting in more detailed and complete works.

Thank you and Happy Reading,

Trina

# Prologue

♥

Calleigh Wells was so glad the sun came out from behind the clouds as she walked down the street. Boston had been experiencing a relentless rainy pattern over the past week. It had been cold, but not enough to turn to snow. She lifted her head to the sky to soak up the burgeoning rays. Now, the temperature was low, but at least, the sun was shining.

She opened the door to Bean Town, her favorite coffee place, and stepped inside. The warm air from the heat flowed over her cheeks, that tingled from the crisp air. Four people stood before her as she weighed a hazelnut latte against a caramel macchiato.

She felt a vibration against her side and opened her purse to see an incoming call on her iPhone. She didn't recognize the out-of-state area code.

"Hello?"

"Is this Mrs. Wells?"

"May I ask who's calling?" She moved forward a step, glancing at the board, she decided to be adventurous on another day. The hazelnut sounded good right then.

"This is Sergeant Cooper. I'm trying to locate Calleigh Wells, wife of Sergeant Kevin Wells."

"Oh God. No." Her heart stuttered, and she couldn't breathe. A military call to her could only have one explanation.

"Mrs. Wells, I regret to inform you that your husband suffered an injury in the line of duty. He is being transferred to Ramstein Air Force base in Germany."

She blindly reached out to keep herself from falling down. When she looked up, she had hold of the man's shirt in front of her. He turned around with a questioning look, but concern replaced it.

"What happened? Is Kevin okay? What—"

"I'm not at liberty to discuss the event. If you wish, I'll put you in contact with his unit liaison. They will make arrangements for you to fly to Germany. Do you have a pen and paper handy?"

"No ... wait... please." She looked at the two men standing side by side in front of her. "Do you have a pen and paper I can borrow?"

The man with black hair held out a pen while the man with auburn hair grabbed a napkin off the counter beside them. Taking the items, she put the phone back up to her ear. "Okay, I'm ready." She wrote the information and ended the call.

She couldn't seem to move. Her feet felt cemented to the floor. She looked around aimlessly, but nothing was in focus. The colors blurred, and her vision swam. She felt herself being guided over to the side and sat in one of the chairs scattered around the room.

The dark-haired man kneeled down in front of her. "Are you okay?" He looked up at his auburn-haired friend, who had pulled the chair out and was resting his hands on her shoulders. Taking her stiff hands between his, the first man rubbed. "Miss? Do we need to get you help?"

His deep voice cut through the haze in her mind. She looked down into a pair of bright sapphire blue eyes. "I need to go home."

"Okay. Did you drive here?"

She shook her head no. Her hands shook so violently, she could barely dial her home number. She held out her phone to the man in front of her. "Can you call? I can't get it to work. My mom can come and get me. She has my babies."

He took the phone from her shaking hands, and handed it to his friend. "Tell you what? Why don't we make things easier on your mom? Conor and I will take you home. I'm Rick." He stopped the woman's head from shaking back and forth by putting a hand to her cheek. "We are completely safe. I promise you. You can talk to your mom the entire way there if you want." He helped her to stand and turned her around so she could see Conor behind her.

"Miss. I think I got the number ye wanted," Conor said, holding out the phone.

She took the phone from the tall man. Blurred vision left her able to decipher only images of red hair and blue-green eyes. She noticed he had some kind of soft lyrical accent. "Thank you."

Putting the phone up to her ear, she heard her mom's voice.

"Mom?" she interrupted. "They called. Kevin's hurt." Tears started slipping down her cheeks. "I'm at Bean Town ... No, I walked...These two men said they'll drive me home." She listened for another minute, then held out the phone to the man with the black hair and blue eyes. "She wants to talk to you."

Rick took the phone from her hand. "Hello? Yes, ma'am. My name is Richard Connor. My friend and I were here at the shop when your daughter got the call. We'll be happy to bring her home. She's in no condition to be out on the streets by herself right now. I assure you we mean her no harm. Can you give me an address?" He listened, then continued, "Okay, we should have her there in about twenty-five minutes." He ended the call and gave back the phone.

Conor walked around to stand next to Rick. "Can ye tell us yer name, miss?"

"It's Calleigh. Calleigh Wells."

"Calleigh, I'm Rick Connor and this is Conor McGuire. Let's get you home to your family." He escorted her to the door Conor held open for them.

They walked half a block down and stopped in front of a dark sedan of some kind. The auburn-haired man opened the front passenger and assisted her into the seat. She sat in silence as he secured the door. She reached for the seatbelt out of habit. They seemed nice, and she was desperate enough to trust two strangers. The window was down a crack and Calleigh heard their voices outside.

"What in the hell just happened?"

"It doesn't sound good. I think somethin' might have happened te her husband or brah'der or somebody. Feck man, she said she had babies at home. I hope to hell 'tis not her husband."

"Yeah, me, too. Let's get out of here. The mother said she lives in Mission Hill."

The two men climbed into the car. She remained silent for several minutes before recognizing her rudeness toward her rescuers. She could worry about her rudeness later. The sergeant on the phone said, injured, not dead. Kevin wasn't dead. It would all be okay. She figured her mom must have given the men directions to the house because they seemed to know where to go.

What are their names again? Rich? Rick? And the other one is Connor?

Wait, *I heard the name Connor twice. I'm sure of it. So who's who?*

She turned to face the man driving, the one with black hair. "Excuse me, but maybe I didn't hear you right. You're both named Connor?" She swiveled around as the auburn-haired one in the backseat laughed.

"That is going to plague us 'til our deaths, man. His last name is Connor. With two 'n's, my first name is Conor, with one. It's how we met. We were on the footie team at B.C. First day of practice, the coach called out 'Connor', and we both answered at the same time. We've been friends ever since."

"I went to B.C. too."

"Always an Eagle," Rick said. "So you said you have children at home?"

She smiled at the thought of her precious little babies. "Yes, I have twin boys. They're two months old." She figured she owed these two some explanation of her erratic behavior. "Their father, my husband, is in the Army Reserve. The phone call was from a sergeant informing me he's injured, but that was all he could tell me. I'm sure he's fine ... right? I mean, if it was serious, they would tell me or send someone or something, wouldn't they?"

Rick watched the beautiful woman next to him. She was looking at him like he had all the answers, and damn, if he wished he didn't. Her honey-blonde hair was pulled back in a ponytail, and her bangs fell over her forehead, ending just above her eyebrows. She had bright brown eyes that looked like gemstones under black sooty lashes. She was a tiny thing, coming just to his chest. The pain and uncertainty in her eyes made all his protective instincts kick in.

"I don't know what military protocol is, but it stands to reason that if things were dire, they would do something other than call you on a cell phone."

He looked at Conor in the rear-view mirror to see if he knew, but saw the man shrug. Conor's dad had been Air Force, stationed in England, before retiring. He wanted to keep Calleigh's hopes alive and distract her mind for right now. "What are your little boys' names?"

"Michael and Brandon. I guess the silver lining is that if Kevin is coming home, he'll be able to meet the boys. He deployed eight months ago, so he's only seen them in pictures and over the internet." She smiled. "They look so much like him. Both have his green eyes and his mouth, but so far they have my blonde hair."

"They sound like *dathuil ógánac*h. I love little kids. Always wanted brothers an' sisters, but not te be."

"Conor, those words. They were beautiful sounding, but I don't understand. What did you say?"

"I said they sound like handsome youth. 'Tis Irish Gaelic. I grew up in Ireland."

"I noticed your accent earlier, but couldn't quite place it."

Rick laughed. "That's because Con's a real mutt. Born in Ireland and lived with his Mom then spent summers in England with his dad. He transferred to the States when he started college, so he's picked up a little American in the past few years. Most people only understand half of what he's talking about. If you get lost, just smile and nod. I do it all the time."

Conor kicked the back of his seat. He laid on the Irish brogue nice and thick, "Ye bloody arse. Stop acting de maggot. Total ballsch ye donna understan' me."

Rick looked over at Calleigh and saw her first genuine smile. It lit up her entire face. He rolled his eyes. "See told you."

Seconds later, they pulled up in front of a quintessential Boston brick row house. The stone base had wrought iron rails leading up the steps, and flower boxes graced the bow windows.

"Wow. Very Nice."

"Yeah, we rent the first and second floors. I have a neighbor in the basement apartment. We got a deal on the place because the owners are army friends of Kevin, stationed overseas." She turned so she could see both men. "Please come in. I'll introduce you to my mom, and you can meet the boys if they're awake."

Rick opened the door and walked around to get Calleigh's, but Conor beat him to it. He looked up, and a woman in her early fifties was standing on the front steps. He guessed she was Calleigh's mom, since they looked like carbon copies of each other. Rick tensed when he inspected the woman's face. Tears streamed down her face. When they walked up the steps, the older woman pulled Calleigh into her arms and held tight.

They all walked inside, but Calleigh stopped dead when a man in uniform stood from the sofa and turned to face her. His face was grim as he held his hat under his arm.

"I'm very sorry, Mrs. Wells. I regret to inform you that your husband Sergeant Kevin Wells—"

"I already received the call of his injury, Captain. What do I do now?"

"Ma'am, there was a miscommunication. Your husband was not injured. He was killed."

Rick and Conor both caught Calleigh as she fell into a heap. Sobs echoed through the room. Her cries of denial ripped into Rick's soul. He wrapped his arm around her, holding her head to his chest. Conor wrapped his around her waist as the heaving shudders racked her small body. They'd only known her for a scant hour, but she'd already wormed her way into his heart. Her clear love of her husband and little boys was a testament to her character. He vowed then and there to protect this woman and her children from that day forward. Looking into Conor's eyes, he knew the man felt the same.

# Chapter One

♥

# Three Years Later

Conor walked into Rick's office and saw that he was on the phone. He settled himself into one of the padded leather chairs, turning the small box in his hand over and over. Inside was their present to Calleigh. Tonight, they would celebrate her twenty-seventh birthday. More importantly, tonight they would begin their quest to make her theirs. It had been three years since the death of her husband. For the first two, they had lived up to their silent vows of that horrible day. They'd become supportive friends to Calleigh and her family.

Helping her through the grief had been difficult, but they'd made a little family of their own with small traditions that helped move the days forward. His favorite was movie night. Every week, one of them would choose a movie, and after she put the boys to bed, they would pile on the living room sofa and watch with all the lights out and an enormous bowl of buttery popcorn in their laps. Usually, Calleigh ended up with her head in one of their laps, sound asleep. He loved to stroke her silky hair or give her foot massages to soothe her after spending all day at her job at the hospital.

Last week, they celebrated Mikey and Bran's third birthday. The boys had gotten to choose the movie, and *Finding Nemo* had swum into the living room in full color. It rattled his cage that the adorable little fish was now considered a Disney classic versus movies he remembered from his childhood. The gigantic eyes and screams of joy when he and Rick carried out a giant cake with all the movie characters printed on it made Conor forget about the quickly passing years.

His head jerked up as Rick hung up the phone and he watched him walk over to sit in the chair opposite him.

"Did you get it?" Rick asked.

He held up the small box. Opening the lid, he showed him the necklace they had designed for Calleigh. The three-stoned pendant featured a bastnäsite with blue sapphire and aquamarine gems on either side.

Rick picked up the box and turned it from side to side, watching the light reflect off the colored gemstones. "Think she'll see the significance?"

"If she doesn't, I'll be happy te point it out te her." Conor smiled.

He looked at Rick and could tell the man was nervous about the taking this next step. Initially, Conor had questioned the decision, but could no longer deny his feelings for Calleigh. Over the past year, the dependable friendship had turned into something much deeper. He wanted the woman like no other. Every time he and Rick brought someone home, he saw the resemblance to the sexy siren who filled their thoughts and made their bodies burn.

Whether they shared a woman or he picked up one on his own, she always had blonde hair and brown eyes, but they never sparkled like Calleigh. At the end of the evening, he felt hollow, sated for the moment but never complete.

"I know yer nervous about changing things between us, but I canny fight it any longer. She's been casually talking about getting back out there more and more. I willna do this without ye, but I love her. Ye love her. We both adore those little boys, like they're our own. It's time we stop bringing home substitutes. It's time we made her ours."

"I know, I know. I want her as bad as you do." Rick ran his hand through his hair. "Fuck, every time in the last year we've had some nameless pickup between us, I've pictured her in our bed. I've even had to hold back crying out her name when I came a time or two."

Conor knew exactly what his best friend was talking about. He'd almost done the same, and more than once, when their eyes had locked in that crucial moment, he'd known they'd both been thinking the same thing. He looked over at Rick's desk as his phone rang again. Jumping up, the man went to answer the summons.

"Rick Connor ... Hey, Calleigh. Happy birthday, angel." He spun around in his chair, catching Conor's eye. "Of course we'll be there for dinner tonight. Six o'clock right?" He laughed. "The boys did what? I can just imagine ... Sure we can talk about it... Okay, see you then." He hung up the phone. "Calleigh said the boys, with grandma's help, made her a huge birthday sign with their handprints painted on it. Unfortunately, the paint didn't get put away, and they decided it needed just a few more decorations. Only it was lying on the sofa."

Conor was laughing so hard he had to clutch his stomach. "Go on otta that!"

"I'm not kidding. You know you have to watch them twenty-four-seven." Rick was laughing, too. After several minutes, he stood and walked over to look out the window of his office. "She said something about wanting our advice at the very end. It sounded serious."

That instantly sobered Conor's mirth. "Feck. I hope nathin' is wrong with the boys."

"No. I don't think so. It sounded more like a personal problem. I hope to hell nobody is haranguing her. If they are, I'll put a stop to that real damn quick." He looked over his shoulder and saw Conor stand then come over next to him. He held out the box in his hand with the lid still open, then put his hand on Rick's shoulder.

"I willna let anything happen to *Ár Ghrá*."

When Rick opened the front door to Calleigh's house, he saw the big sign the boys had made for her. The boys' solo addition of green stripes stood out against the little blue handprints.

"Hello?" he called out.

Two little voices yelled out, then it sounded as if a herd of buffalo were running down the hallway. He turned toward the commotion and two leg-latching spider monkeys tackled him. "Why if it isn't the deadly duo."

He scooped up a boy in each arm. He looked at Brandon and said, "Mikey, did you tell your mommy happy birthday?" Peals of laughter rang over his ears, and Brandon pointed at his brother, shaking his head.

"I not Mikey."

"Are you sure you're not Mikey? I think you two are trying to trick us again."

Conor came over and took the real Mikey from Rick. "I know how te tell them apart." He lifted his hand high in the air in the shape of a claw. Wiggling his fingers on the way down, he made like he was going to tickle the little boy.

Mikey started laughing and squirming in Conor's arms. Brandon kept pointing at his brother, and merriment danced in his dark green eyes.

"See works every time. Mikey is ticklish," Conor said.

Rick looked at Brandon. "I'm still not convinced. We may have a couple of doppelgangers on our hands. Let me try." He swooped in and started tickling his stomach.

Brandon began squirming and laughing the same as his brother. "Well, it looks like we have two Mikeys on our hands."

Calleigh walked into the room. "What's going on in here? It sounds like a bunch of monkeys live in my house."

Rick put Brandon down at the same time Conor put down Mike. The two boys ran back down the hall to their playroom.

"No running," all three adults yelled.

Rick walked over to Calleigh. Gathering her close, he kissed her the on the temple. "Happy birthday, angel."

He still had Calleigh in his arms when Conor came up behind her.

Conor placed his hands on Calleigh's waist, above Rick's arms, and leaned down to her ear. "*Breithlá shona duit, muirnín.*" Then he kissed her temple on the opposite side Rick had.

Rick watched Calleigh's eyes close and felt a shiver travel down her body. It appeared to be from arousal, not nerves. This was the first time they had intentionally put her between them. He smiled inwardly at her reaction. When she opened her eyes, he gasped at the desire he saw for a split second before they changed back to their normal glow.

She turned from Rick's arms and faced Conor. "I love it when you speak Gaelic. Of course, for all I know, you're insulting me, but it sounds so pretty."

He switched holds with Rick. "Never. I said 'Happy Birthday, sweetheart'. We have a gift for ye. Would ye like it now or after dinner?"

She peered down the hall. "I don't hear any crashes or yelling. I put on a cartoon for them shortly before you arrived, so they're probably content for the moment. We'd better do it now, while they're distracted. Come with me into the kitchen. I have to stir the sauce."

As they walked down the hall, Rick peeked into the playroom. Both boys' heads turned, and they smiled, but remained seated on the floor. He winked at them, and like little mirrors, they blinked both eyes back, trying to imitate him. He chuckled, then followed Calleigh and Conor into the kitchen. After Calleigh stirred the spaghetti sauce, he lifted her to sit on the counter.

"Rick! What if the boys come in? This is hardly setting a good example."

"They're fine, but if you insist." He lifted her back into his arms and sat down in a chair at the table, keeping her on his lap. "How's this?"

"Ye just wanted te carry her around." Conor said, pulling out the necklace box they'd tied a white ribbon to.

He shrugged unapologetically and pulled Calleigh a little closer. She took the box from Conor and eased the bow loose. The snap of the hinge was a prelude to a burst of pure happiness; her gasp of wonder was a melody to his ears.

"Oh wow! You guys, this is so beautiful." She looked down at the three colored stones, then back up into the smiling faces of her best friends. "It's us, right? The blue, brown, and aqua?"

"See, I told ye she would figure it out," Conor said. He undid the clasp and attached it behind Calleigh's neck. "There. Looks perfect against ye skin."

Calleigh was going nuts being held by Rick, while Conor attached their gift. His fingers caressed her skin as he traced the chain down to the pendant. He was so close she could feel his breath puff against her neck. Rick's arm was around her waist, and every once in a while, his fingers would caress her side. This was new behavior. Never had the two men surrounded her like tonight. Their body heat and scent wrapped around her like a cocoon. She so wanted to close her eyes and swim in the forgotten sensations, but knew the boys would soon chant for dinner. She linked her fingers with Rick's and moved his arm so she could stand.

Stepping away, she caught a look shared between her two best friends. They both had little smiles on their faces and each slightly nodded his head. She bent over to grab a large bowl in the cabinet by her feet and could have sworn she heard one of them groan. She flipped off the switch on the stove and lifted the heavy pot of boiling water to drain the noodles.

She'd told Rick on the phone earlier that she wanted to talk to them about something. She had intended to tell them she'd accepted her first date since Kevin's death and wanted some advice on getting back into the dating scene.

She remained dazed for the year following Kevin's death. She'd been able to function and take care of the boys, but it seemed as if the only emotion she could express outside of being a mother in love with her burgeoning babies was pain.

The day Brandon and Mikey had taken their first steps; Rick and Conor had been there. All three of them had cheered and encouraged the tentative steps towards independence. That was the day she'd woken up and found that the two men who had rescued her on the blackest of days were still there. Not only were they there, but she'd become dependent on their support. So many nights she'd cried in their arms only to find peace once the tears passed. Now she wanted more. She wanted to feel a woman's pleasure again. She wanted to feel a man's desire, and on the darkest of nights in the silence of her bedroom, she'd dreamed of the tangled limbs and sweat-slicked bodies of three.

Ménage wasn't foreign to her. When she and Kevin were in college, they had invited a third to their bed frequently. They had a circle of friends who were trustworthy and treated the experience with respect and honor. Everyone in the circle knew that the third was only a participant in the sex. The friends understood they would stay out of their partners' relationships.

Looking over her shoulder, she saw Rick and Conor whispering to each other. She couldn't hear what they were saying, though. Their behaviors suggested a familiarity with having a woman between them, but she'd heard nothing about them sharing before. She knew they dated, hell they were both stunning specimens. Both men had kept the athletic bodies of their college soccer days. Neither bulged with muscle, but their bodies were hard, trim and defined.

A few months ago, she recognized the signs of physical attraction to her two best friends. If Rick and Conor's presence reawakened her body, then she supposed the time to date again had come. She figured she would start out slow and see what happened. As much as she'd recognized her desire for Rick and Conor, she didn't want to risk losing them over her awakening hormones. She refused to choose one over the other.

They were fixtures in the house on a weekly basis. The boys looked upon them as father figures, even if they didn't quite understand that yet. They always obeyed Rick and Conor as much as they did her. As much as three-year-olds obeyed anyone. Brandon and Mikey were eager to show the men a prize drawing they had done that day, told them stories of their adventures together, and even started asking for an occasional bedtime story. Rick and Conor had been there for every milestone. They were even helping with the potty training as much as they could. They were parents in all ways except having an intimate relationship with her.

She'd accepted the date with Miles from the hospital, where she was a nurse anesthetist, because Rick and Conor were out of her league and off-limits in her mind. But what if they weren't? What if they wanted to take their relationship to the next level, and what if they wanted to do it together? Her pulse raced at the possibility, and she felt dampness between her legs that hadn't been there since before the boys were born.

After dinner, Rick and Conor took the boys upstairs for baths and bed while she cleaned the kitchen. The nights they came over ran more efficiently. The four extra hands at bedtime made things run a lot smoother. She saw them come down the stairs about forty-five minutes later.

"They tucked in?" she asked.

Rick nodded. "Yeah, go on up and give them a kiss goodnight."

She did, and when she came back down, they were both sprawled on the sofa watching the news. Taking her customary place between them, she sighed and relaxed into the deep cushions. A damp spot remained from the earlier paint cleaning, but she ignored it. As she toyed with her new necklace, Conor put his arm around her shoulder and Rick placed his large hand on her thigh. She absorbed the heat from their touch, and her muscles relaxed even further.

"So, are you working on any cool new games?"

They both worked in the sports division for a major video game company. Rick was a game designer, and Conor a software engineer. Frequently, they told her about new games they were working on, and she'd even gotten pre-releases for the Xbox they'd bought last year. She had laughed so hard when they said it was for the boys with such innocent expressions on their faces. Because two-year-olds needed the latest gaming system. Of course, they had promptly set up the system and played for hours that night.

Rick turned to look at Calleigh. "I just got the proposal for a new game. It's going to feature famous Olympic athletes and their sports. We'll release it when the next games begin. Calleigh, you mentioned needing to speak with us tonight. What's going on?"

She worried her bottom lip between her teeth for a moment. She couldn't avoid this conversation, but she was curious about their reaction to her news after their earlier chemistry. Standing, she turned to include both men in her line of vision before sitting on the large ottoman in front of the sofa.

"Well, the thing is, I have a date." She waited to see their reactions. Both men's eyes darkened, but their outward expression didn't change.

Conor's hands fisted into the sofa but he said, "I'm glad yer getting back out there. Is it someone we know?"

She shook her head. "His name is Miles, and he works at the hospital with me. He's a radiology technician. I met him in the cafeteria a few weeks back. We've eaten together a few times. He's a nice enough guy."

Rick sat up straight and rested his elbows on his knees as he leaned in closer to Calleigh. "Angel, I'm glad you feel you're ready to date again, but what do you know about this guy? Have you talked to any other staff who know him? What if he's a complete jerk? What if he only wants to get in your pants?"

"*Muirnín*. I donna want ye doin' a line with some paddy who just wants te shag ye."

Calleigh could tell despite their calm faces, they were upset. When riled up, Conor always spoke with a thicker accent and used more colloquialisms. Rick got stoic, and right now, his face appeared as if it were a wooden mask.

She kneeled on the floor and took hold of a hand from each man. "I appreciate your concern. I even love you for it. But it's time for me to try this again. Don't worry so much. The two of you have spoiled me so rotten over the past three years that I have impossibly high standards. I'm sure we'll just go to dinner, and I'll be home before eleven o'clock."

She leaned in and kissed each one of them on the cheek, letting the little caress linger a tad longer than usual. "I know this is a lot to ask, especially given your misgivings, but would you be willing to watch Mike and Brandon that night?"

"Of course we will. I plan on being here when he drops you off to make sure he behaves like a gentleman," Rick said, looking over to see Conor nodding in agreement.

# Chapter Two

♥

Rick paced the living room, waiting for Calleigh to get home from her date. Normally he'd watch the late night news, but he was too keyed. Thinking about that other man touching her, holding her hand, or God forbid kissing her, was driving him nuts. He heard Conor come down the stairs after checking on the boys, again. He could tell the man was just as much of a wreck. As Rick turned to face the front windows, he saw a car pull into the open spot in front of the house. Conor must have caught the direction of his gaze because he sprinted past him to peer out the curtain.

"Conor, get away from there!" Rick said, walking that same direction.

"Go an' shoite." He pulled the curtain back just enough to peek around the corner. "*Damnú ort Bualadh craicinn Bastún!*"

Rick stomped over to the window to stand behind Conor. "I have no idea what you just said, but it didn't sound pleasant. Let me see."

"The fecking gobshite is practically ridin' her!"

"Move, Con!" he hissed, looking out the window. "Goddamn fucking bastard is practically giving her a tonsillectomy!"

"That's what I said," Conor murmured.

"Yeah, but nobody can ever understand you when you get riled up."

He pulled Conor away from the window before Calleigh caught sight of them. Moments later, he heard the key turn in the lock at the front door. He hoped like hell she would not bring what's his name inside. He might have a hard time restraining himself from punching the man.

"Conor, get your ass over here."

He flipped on the news and pretended to watch. Conor flopped down on the sofa just before the latch opened. Rick heard Calleigh say goodnight and released the breath he'd been holding. A few seconds later, she was between them, where she belonged, but her expression didn't reflect a blissful kiss. He did a little happy dance inside.

"How was the date?" Conor asked.

Calleigh heaved out a breath. "It was okay. He was polite. Made all the right conversation. Even kissed me, but it felt like his tongue was a tentacle. No spark. Nothing. Maybe I'm not ready after all."

She looked disillusioned. Rick knew fire burned inside her. It just needed the right spark to ignite. He looked at Conor and saw him nod. He turned Calleigh's head towards him. His hand tunneled in the silky mass of her honey-blonde hair. Her amber-brown eyes darkened as he leaned his head forward. He touched their lips together for the first time. She tasted of cherry as he flicked his tongue out to taste. Her mouth opened, and he slipped inside, moaning at his first real taste of Calleigh.

Her mouth was sweet and welcoming. He turned his head to get a better angle and sealed them together tighter. His mouth moved on hers in a slow rhythm. Her tongue came out to play with his and slipped into his mouth as his retreated from hers. He became hard and aching. His hand moved lower to caress her breast, only to find Conor's already there. He pulled back and looked into her passion-dazed eyes. Conor's hand cupped her cheek and turned her head toward him.

Rick watched their lips meet and fuse. Their mouths moved together in perfect synchronicity. Rick cupped her breast in his hand and molded the full mound. Her nipple was erect and stabbing his palm. He slid his other hand up underneath the hem of her dress, touching and caressing the soft skin of her inner thigh. Her legs opened a little, and he angled his fingers up to touch the edge of her panties. He skimmed the fabric, but didn't reach underneath. Conor's mouth swallowed little moans and cries as he continued to lick and devour Calleigh's plush lips.

It always made him hot to see Conor pleasuring the women they'd chosen to bring home, but knowing that this was Calleigh, their Calleigh, made the experience ten times more erotic. Conor loved to kiss. One of his preferred activities. He would kiss them all over for hours, while Rick was more of a touch person. He loved the feel of a woman between them, touching her skin and slipping his fingers inside her body. His cock inside the snug, wet heat of a pussy or the hot, velvet clasp of an ass could melt his brain. Add Conor into the mix, filling the woman's mouth or other available opening, and his mind exploded. Hearing the screams of her pleasure echo in the room, feeling the rake of her nails down his back, was the best feeling in the world. They would have that with Calleigh, and they would have that soon.

Calleigh pulled back from Conor and looked over at Rick on the other side of her. "Holy shit," she whispered. "Umm, guys? What was that all about?"

"Did ye get yer fireworks, *Ár Ghra*?" Conor asked

"More like a nuclear explosion. But I don't understand. Since when..."

"Since when have we wanted you, angel, or since when have we shared our women?"

Judging by her expression, Calleigh weighed his questions. Was she in shock that they wanted her, or that they intended to share her? The lust coursing through his system muddled his thoughts. Calleigh had responded to their touch with pure passion. Both his and Conor's. He didn't want her to feel overwhelmed, and maybe he and Conor should have approached her individually, but Rick didn't want there to be any confusion or turmoil for his angel. He felt certain that he and Conor, individually, exerted powerfully addictive charms—their combined seduction defied calculation. Calleigh was precious. She wasn't some experiment to get their rocks off. There needed to be clarity and consent for the future he envisioned to become a reality.

"Why don't we start with since when have you wanted me?"

Rick looked at Conor. "You want to take this one?"

Conor took Calleigh's hand between his. "The desire te make ye mine began a little over a year ago. 'Til then, I was happy being yer friend, yer confidant, yer shoulder te cry on. I canny mind a specific day it changed. I started lookin' forward te yer smiles. The little touches ye gave made me shiver. I started dreaming of ye at night. Since Rick and I live together, he called me on it. When I admitted the truth, he told me he felt the same." He looked over at Rick, "Yer turn."

"We started sharing women back in college. We were roommates for four years. The first time was junior year. I had a girl over and Conor came back to the room after studying at the library. He didn't realize I had company and walked in on us. The girl at the time was rather ... we'll say ... free with her affections. She invited Conor to join us. It was then that we recognized the power of pleasing a woman in tandem. Working together to provide a woman with pleasure unequaled to her previous experience not only enhances her satisfaction but ours as well."

"Do you always share? Are the women convenient thirds, or is this a lifestyle you've adopted permanently?"

"Not every time. We do date on our own, but more often than not, we're together. Five years ago, we decided that ultimately we are happier this way. There is something about making a woman scream with rapture. Watching her eyes wild and desperate for the release only the two of us can give. I enjoy watching Conor fuck with his drive and determination to bring a woman the most intense orgasm possible. I enjoy sinking myself deep inside a tight pussy or ass, knowing that he is there, stimulating her body in ways I couldn't do in that moment of time." Rick laced his fingers together with Calleigh's. "We want to live as a throuple with one special woman permanently. We want a marriage of three. As friends, Conor and I balance each other out. I can't imagine living my life without his presence surrounding me every day. I need him. I love him. However, I'm not in love with him. We need to complete the triangle. We need a woman to love, to cherish, to protect." He cupped her cheek and placed a soft kiss on her lips. "We need you, angel. You and the boys have become our world. We want to marry you, be fathers to Michael and Brandon and have future children with you. We also want to see you fly from passion, see you burn from our touch, feel your soft skin between us and know the ecstasy of being inside your body."

Rick's dark description of their passion for ménages had her light-headed. She wanted to feel them surround her as he'd described. The two men she thought she knew inside and out had hidden depths. She knew they each had a tremendous capacity to love, and they worked as a team, but seeing them in this new light was a revelation. They wanted to build a life with one woman as their wife. As the mother of their children. While she had experience of three in the bedroom, she didn't know how a marriage of three would work. How would they interact daily? How would relationships between the individuals grow? When they fought, would they have to draw sides? Calleigh didn't know if she could do that.

"I can see that we've thrown a lashing of information at ye the-nite, *muirnín*. The necklace we gave ye was our way of telling ye our desires te build a new relationship between the three of us. We want ye te take the next few days te think about it. We know ye have te think of the boys, not only yer wants an' needs. I think ye know that we already love Mike an' Brandon as our own. We don't want to replace their owl lad, but we do want te fill the hole his death left in all ye lives."

Calleigh stood and walked them to the front door. She stopped before opening it and leaned into Conor. Reaching up on her toes, she wrapped her arms around his neck and lifted her head for another kiss. His hands dropped to her waist to steady her as his mouth descended. His lips were warm and firm, his tongue soft as it entered her mouth. Instantly, her skin heated and her blood rushed through her veins. The man knew how to kiss. Little flicks kept her searching for deeper contact. His lips pulled away, only to tease and torment before capturing hers again. His hands practically spanned her waist. She imagined being lifted by his solid arms and wrapping her legs around his lean waist as he thrust inside her. His hard body against hers felt so good. It felt right. His erection pushed against her stomach. The hard column of flesh was long and thick. He wrapped his arms around her back and pulled her into his body so no space separated them.

Another pair of hands lifted her hair away from her neck, and lips touched her neck. The delicate caress countered Conor's thrusting tongue. Rick's tongue traced her pulse and nipped behind her ear.

They surrounded her with their heat. The intensity of their touches was overpowering. Rick's deep voice whispered seductive words in her ear and planted images of the three of them entwined on her bed, arms and legs touching, lips meeting, bodies sliding and thrusting together until their passions consumed them. His hands came around and cupped her breasts. His thumbs and fingers pulled on her elongated nipples. The stiff peaks were aching and needy. She tilted her head away from Conor's and leaned back on Rick's chest.

His head descended and their lips met in a backward kiss, melting together. Conor kissed her bare shoulders and down the neckline of her dress. His tongue flicked out to catch the inner swell of her breasts, and she moaned into Rick's mouth. Conor's deep voice purred in her ear. His lyrical accent was thick with passion. Although she didn't understand the Gaelic, his reverent tone implied words filled with desire and longing. Finally, the three separated, each of them breathing hard. The two men couldn't hide the arousal that matched hers. She wanted them to finish what they started, but her brain knew there were things to consider before they took that irrevocable step.

She turned and placed her hand on Rick's cheek, stretching up for one last chaste kiss. "Goodnight, Rick."

He pulled her into a tight hug. "Goodnight, angel."

She did the same to Conor. "Goodnight, Conor."

He pulled Calleigh into his arms. "*Oíche mhaith, muirnín*. Goodnight, sweetheart."

As she closed the door, she thought if they continued in this relationship; she was definitely going to learn some Gaelic. She walked up the stairs and peeked in on the boys. Their flayed-out limbs on their twin beds caused her to smile. She, Rick, and Conor had made a big production of going to the 'big boy' bed store on the boys' third birthday. Mike and Brandon had picked out their own bedding. A space theme filled their room, complete with glow-in-the-dark stars, and their chosen bed set featured stitched rockets, comets, planets, and stars. They'd also picked out their own potty seats, and so far, things seemed to be working out well ... mostly. She leaned over and gave each of her sons a kiss on the forehead and smelled the baby shampoo from their baths Rick and Conor had given them earlier.

Closing the door, she made her way into her bedroom. Stripping off her dress, she decided a warm bath would soothe her before going to bed. She didn't have an ensuite, and the bathroom was next to the boys' room, but she'd always been fortunate that once down, her duo slept hard. Calleigh padded her way to the bathroom in her robe. She turned on the taps; the water gurgling as the tub filled. With a practiced hand, she added coarse sea salts and iridescent oil beads, their scent already filling the air. When that little stick turned blue, the last thing Calleigh imagined was becoming a single mother.

She was so fortunate that her salary at the hospital, in combination with the compensation payments from Kevin's service-related death, allowed her the income to support her family. Her village also included her mother and of course, Rick and Conor. While parenthood was truly a matter of trial and error, Calleigh felt they all succeeded more often than failed. The hot water surrounding her was luxuriant. The moisture washed away the stress of the day. Her muscles went lax, and she closed her eyes.

Mikey and Bran were growing up so fast. If she agreed to Rick and Conor's proposal, her babies would have more than transient father figures. Calleigh had no concerns about the boys' relationship with Rick and Conor. The twins adored her best friends, and the feelings were one hundred percent mutual. So what was it that held her back? Nerves about being intimate again? Fear of commitment? Rick and Conor made it abundantly clear that the relationship they proposed was one of permanence. Was she willing to risk her heart? Her body was on board, but her soul had been shattered once before, and Calleigh didn't know if she could survive another catastrophe. But being in Rick and Conor's arms was the first time she'd felt alive in years.

Images of aroused Rick and Conor floated behind her eyelids. Rick's eyes darkened from their normal bright sapphire blue to navy. With his lighter coloring, slashes of color popped up on Conor's cheekbones. She had felt the press of both men's erections against her body, the pressure of the thick bulges against her stomach melting her core. She still felt their hands on her breasts and their fingers pulling at her nipples.

Lifting her hands out of the water, she cupped her swollen mounds and milked the turgid peaks. Spikes of desire streamed down her body to her clit, and she moaned. Reaching down, she slipped the fingers of one hand between the plump folds of her pussy. Using her first finger, she circled her clit. She rolled the little bundle of nerves a few times before flicking it with her nail. Sliding down, she gathered some moisture from her channel to bring it back up. A warm, buoyant embrace of water surrounded her, the rhythmic lapping a gentle caress that filled her with pleasure. Her finger continued to circle her clit, while her other hand pinched the nipple she'd played with. The slight sting quickly morphed from pain to euphoria. She dipped her fingers inside her channel. Wetness coated her fingers and the soft plush tissues gripped tight around her. It had been a long time since she had anything more than a couple of fingers inside her.

How would it feel to be stretched around Rick's or Conor's thick cocks? The burn as they entered her unused muscles, the long columns of flesh reaching deep inside her? Her fingers pumped but were too small to reach the depths she really needed. Pulling out, she concentrated on her clit. It was Rick's head between her legs. His tongue lashing at the protrusion, sucking it between his lips and occasionally scraping his teeth across it. Her fingers tried to mimic the sensations by circling around and pushing down, flicking her nail on the underside. She felt her orgasm closing in.

Sticking the first finger of her other hand back inside her pussy, she coated it with moisture, then reached below to circle the small rosette of her back opening. She imagined it was Conor stimulating the tight opening and moaned his name. She slipped it inside up to the second knuckle, then placed a thumb at the dripping center of her core. Any second now, she was going to come. She pushed both fingers as deep as they would go and pinched them together to rub on the thin membrane separating the two spaces.

Her body erupted as she cried out their names.

# Chapter Three

It had been three days since they informed Calleigh of their desires. Rick was eager to get to the house after work to see how she was processing things. He was sure she would have some questions for them. After shutting down his laptop, he locked up his office to meet Conor in the lobby of their building. When he got there, the man was already pacing.

"What took ye so long?"

"Con, it's only five after. Settle down, okay. I'm sure things are fine. You saw how she responded to us the other night. If she has any misgiving, I'm sure it'll be about the boys, and I don't see that as insurmountable."

"You're right. I'm sorry. Let's just go." He walked out the lobby doors and turned towards the T station nearby.

Twenty minutes later, they were at Calleigh's front door. Rick opened the portal and stuck his head inside. "Hello?"

He heard Calleigh's voice from the kitchen, telling them to come back. He and Conor walked through the living room and into the bright, friendly space. Calleigh was lifting warm chocolate chip cookies off a baking sheet. They were his favorites, and he was determined to steal one.

"Angel, you didn't have to bake me cookies." He reached over and tried to snag one, but got his hand slapped with the spatula.

"Hands off, cookie monster." She looked over her shoulder with a smile.

He looked over his shoulder to see Conor snickering. "What are you laughing at, you mick?"

"Ye, pouting like a babby because ye canny have a cookie. Fer bleedin' sake the boys are better behaved than ye."

With a saucy smile, Calleigh picked up an oatmeal raisin, Conor's favorite, and sauntered over, holding it out to him.

"Are you hungry, Conor?"

He smiled. "I've a mouth on me." He accepted the treat and moaned at the first bite.

"Hey! Why does he get one, and I don't?"

"Because you get this..."

Calleigh wrapped her hand around his neck. She lifted on her toes, and he met her head halfway. Their lips met, and his insides soared.

*She's ours!*

Cupping his hands underneath her ass, he lifted her and swung around the kitchen in circles. Calleigh's legs wrapped around his waist, and he held her close to him, not wanting to break their connection. She felt so good. Her small body held in his arms, her soft curves pressed against his chest.

He opened his eyes to see Conor's gaze riveted on the sight of them. Their blue-green orbs were bright, and the telltale slashes of color across his cheeks gave away his desire. Rick set her down on Conor's lap at the kitchen table, so he could get his acceptance kiss. Their mouths met, Conor's hand holding the back of Calleigh's neck to keep her close. Calleigh's arms coiled around Conor's neck, holding him tight. Watching them kiss, Rick's cock hardened even more. Their heads finally lifted.

"Does this mean what I hope it does?" Rick asked.

"Yes, I want to be yours. I know there are some logistical things to work out, and I don't know exactly how a marriage of three works. My only experience with ménage was when Kevin would invite a third to our bed, but I've never tried to have a full relationship with more than two."

Rick swallowed at Calleigh's confession. He did not know that she'd experienced ménage before. "You and Kevin used to..."

She adjusted her position on Conor's lap, turning so she could lean against his chest and face Rick. "Sometimes. Back when we were in college. Mostly, I know what I'm getting into, and I can honestly say I can't think of two men I want more."

Rick looked over Calleigh's head at Conor, who seemed just as shocked as he was, but then a huge smile lit up his face and Rick mirrored it. Their woman was full of wonderful surprises. He had to admit a slight disappointment at not being the ones to introduce her to the intensity of a threesome, but having experience meant that she would know whatever explosive feelings occurred were a product of the three of them, not the newness of the situation.

He stalked her from across the room. Her words setting him on fire. He was harder than a spike and wanted nothing more than to sink into her desirable body. "God almighty, Calleigh. I need you. I want to feel you between us. I want to hear your screams of pleasure. I want to sink so deep inside we can't tell where I stop and you begin. When are the boys being dropped off?"

She was breathing hard and wiggled against Conor's crotch. "Not enough time tonight for the full five courses, but I think we can do an appetizer."

"*Muirnín*, yer gonna slay me with that sweet mouth."

Rick kneeled in front of Calleigh and Conor. He undid the drawstring of her scrubs from the hospital. Conor lifted her by the waist while Rick pulled down the pants and her underwear, revealing the silky skin of her mound. She had a small strip of hair, but most of the area was bare. He saw moisture slick and dewy coating the lips, and his mouth watered for a taste. Conor lifted her shirt to bare her breasts. His fingers rasped and pulled at her nipples. Rick leaned in and flicked his tongue around and across the peaks. They were large and plush; the areolas encompassing several inches of her full breasts. Calleigh's head leaned back against Conor's chest, but her eyes opened to watch Rick. Her eyes glazed over with a dazed expression, and her pupils dilated. Rick was aware of the time constraints but committed to making sure Calleigh savored every bit of her awakening passion.

He separated her legs, and Conor reached down to hold them open. Rick circled her navel with his tongue several times. His teeth nipped at the sensitive flesh, then soothed tiny bites with slow licks. He put his nose to her belly and breathed warm moist air on the skin as he dragged it down to the top of her pussy. He placed little kisses all along the outer edges. His hands glided up from her knees until they reached the top.

"You're wet, Calleigh. I'm going to taste this lovely cream."

He used his thumbs to spread open her swollen lips. He stroked through the moist folds, and her taste exploded over his tongue. The sweet musky flavor was nectar in his mouth. He alternated long and firm upward strokes with dips inside the clasping heat of her core.

"Oh God, Rick. It's been so long. Please don't stop." She panted.

He felt the muscles clench around his tongue and knew she was close. He looked up to see Conor's eyes burning at the sight of Rick's mouth fastened to Calleigh. His hands had released her legs and were pinching and rolling her nipples again, stimulating the sensitive peaks. Calleigh's sweet little cries for more echoed in the kitchen. She bucked her hips up, searching for a greater connection.

"Don't worry, angel. I won't stop until you're screaming for us."

Rick slid two fingers inside her in one smooth thrust. The fiery heat scorched his skin, and the tight muscles clenched around the digits. She spasmed around his fingers, every ripple of her flesh embracing him. She was overwhelming tight. He wondered if she's had anything inside her since before her husband had passed.

Gasping cries poured from her throat as she arched, legs tightening, back bowing against Conor's chest. The cream of her response soaked Rick's fingers. He leaned down, closed his lips over her clit and sucked hard while thrusting deep inside and massaging the hypersensitive nerves. He heard her gasp, felt her muscles lock down, and a surge of warmth spilled into his hand as she climaxed.

Calleigh's eyes unfurled as Conor eased her down from the explosive orgasm. She wanted to be fucked. She needed it, now. Rick and Conor had awakened her body, and it demanded the feel of a hard cock pushing deep. The orgasm Rick had given her had been fantastic, best in a long time, but she needed to be filled. Rick, on his knees at her feet, had opened his trousers and caressed his cock. The long, thick stalk was red and dripping with desire. She wanted a taste. She wanted to feel the thickness slide deep down her throat.

She slid out of Conor's lap and landed on her hands and knees in front of him. Her head hung limp, poised over the crown of his cock, her long hair falling around to create a curtain. She panted over the top as Rick dragged his fist up and down. One of his hands came up to rest on top of her head, and he guided her down in obvious invitation. Her tongue came out and licked across the top, catching the drop of pre-cum oozing from his wide slit.

"Oh angel. I'll give you one hundred years to stop that."

She opened her mouth to take the first several inches inside. Her tongue swirled around the crown as she pulled up, working the head with her lips. Rick's hands threaded through her hair and tugged at the strands. She heard a chair scrape across the hardwood floor and the heat of Conor's body was behind her.

Seconds later, she felt a pressure at her opening. He seemed huge and hot. Conor eased his way inside her channel. The head of his cock stretching the narrow space. It burned a little, but felt so damn good. Exciting.

She pushed back, demanding more. She wanted all of him. He was hot and hard, and she could scarcely stand the teasing. He stopped when the first couple of inches were inside her, and they both paused. Rick imprisoned her head in his hands. Conor gripped her hips, preventing her from pushing backward onto his cock. What were they waiting for? She needed them. She needed to be taken. Desperation to feel both their bodies fill hers made her whimper. Rick's large hands held her head captive, preventing her from looking up. She couldn't use her hands on him because they were holding her up. Trying to incite them to move, she whipped her tongue all around the head of his cock. It filled her mouth. She didn't know if she could take the entire length into her throat, but would damn well try her best.

As if on a timer, they both moved forward and filled her body simultaneously. Her scream and their moans mingled together. She felt the fullness of Rick's cock in her mouth, while Conor's length stretched deep inside her.

"*Naofa damnú air! Go mboga mé!*"

"English, Conor. You want us to understand you, speak English. That's it, baby. Take me deep. All the way to your throat." He hissed as she moved further down and swallowed.

"Holy shite! I have te move!" Conor pulled back and thrust inside in one long, smooth stroke. "Goddamn Rick, you've never felt anythin' like this. Her cream is so hot an' wet, it feels like movin' through liquid silk."

They moved in practiced rhythm. At first, one would pull out of her as the other pushed in. Then they both filled her concurrently. Over and over. She trembled with arousal. Rick was driving his cock deep into her mouth. She tried to swallow whenever it reached the back, wanting to give him the most stimulation possible. Conor was fucking her in long, deep thrusts. A smooth slide into her body, followed by the rough retreat. The pace increased. Her brain shut down, and she was along for the mind-bending ride on a wave a bliss. She recalled similar sensations from a time long ago, but nothing compared to the feel of Rick and Conor inside her.

Her body countered their rhythm, moving down on Rick's cock as Conor pulled back and pushing into Conor's thrusts as she sucked up Rick's length. She heard moans and cries and realized they came from her.

Her body was on the brink of combustion. Her blood was on fire as it raced through her veins. She clenched around Conor and heard him cry out behind her. Rick was thrusting fast and deep into her throat. They were taking her. Her men were claiming their mate, and it was the most incredible thing she had ever experienced. God help her when one of them filled her ass and the other her pussy. She might not survive.

"*Chan fhad'thuige*! I'm gonna come. *Tá mé chomh mór sin i ngrá leat*. Ye burn me alive ye feel so perfect surroundin' me."

"I'm almost there, angel. I'm going to come deep in your throat. Conor's going to shoot, too. I can tell he's close. He only starts speaking that much Gaelic when his brain melts down."

Her orgasm was building deep in her womb. The contractions spread outward to consume her entire body. Both men thrust faster, and a few moments later, she felt the first shots of Rick's cum hit her tongue. She let the salty taste linger before swallowing everything he had. The feel of him releasing inside her triggered a second, more explosive climax in her. She screamed around him as her body convulsed. Conor thrust hard, then held still deep inside her. She felt him swell even thicker, and his cock pulsed. His fingers gripped her hips as he yelled out her name.

Rick pulled out of her mouth, and her arms collapsed. She ended up in a heap on the floor with Conor still buried deep inside, his arms braced out so he didn't crush her. He rolled to his side and withdrew from her body. Rick promptly scooped her up into his arms, and Conor scooted against her back to hold her tight between them.

"I think that was the single best moment of my life," Rick whispered.

Her body still trembled with aftershocks. As much as she wanted to curl up with her men, she knew the boys would be home soon.

"We have to get up."

Twin groans echoed above her head.

"I know I don't want to either, but Bran and Mikey will be home soon."

They helped her to stand and slip her scrub bottoms back on. Both men righted their trousers.

She went upstairs to change into jeans and a soft sweater. The material sliding over her still sensitive skin caused goose bumps to rise on her arms. As she left her bedroom, she heard the front door open and twin exclamations of excitement. She smiled at the joyful sound of her boys. A profound love bound them to Rick and Conor.

Two days later, the three of them went out on their first official date. Conor and Rick took Calleigh to dinner at an upscale restaurant, then they wanted to take her somewhere exciting and fun. It had been a long time since the three of them had gone out to play. A popular piano bar in Back Bay seemed like the perfect idea. The staff seated them at the table, and immediately, the dueling pianos began. Playing classic rock songs as the whole place sang along. An electric fiddle player even got on stage and performed an amazing rendition of *Devil*

*Went Down to Georgia*. Strobe lights flashed as he stood on top of the pianos and wailed on the strings.

After an hour, Conor brought some drinks back from the bar for all three of them. Between the pianos and the crowd, the noise in the bar was so loud he had trouble hearing his thoughts. But where normally an environment like that would have him giving Rick a pleading look to vacate, tonight he enjoyed soaking up the atmosphere. Calleigh was stunning and even through the cacophony, her laughter was music to his ears. And Rick's bright smile radiated glee as he wrapped his arms around Calleigh and kissed her temple.

Conor set the drinks down, then leaned over to whisper in Rick's ear. "I have gotta little surprise for our girl."

He tried to keep his expression neutral, but Rick's sharp gaze missed nothing.

"What did you do?"

"Dinna worry ye will love it. Ye mind senior year when we went te that place in Allston?"

"Yeah ... oh shit... you didn't!"

Rick's laughter made several people at a nearby table glance in their direction. Conor toasted them with his tumbler of whiskey, and the party all raised their glasses in return. He took a sip as he leaned against the wall. The Irish whiskey wasn't his preferred brand, but for a bar in Boston, it sufficed. Conor knew he was a bit of an alcohol snob. He loved a full-bodied burgundy, and the smoothness of his homeland's triple distilled heritage. As the whiskey warmed his belly, his skin craved Calleigh's touch. He moved closer to his date, and the light scent of Calleigh's perfume and the sparkle in her eyes was like a siren call. Conor shifted his glass to the other hand and wrapped an arm around their woman's waist. He angled his body so that his touch wasn't obvious to the crowd.

Several years ago when he and Rick decided living and loving in a throuple was their lifelong intention, they came up with a system for group dates. One of them would take the lead for displays of affection and social interaction regarding the relationship and the other a supporting role. They didn't keep score or take turns, and the supporting partner didn't refrain from interaction, but they'd found the system worked well and kept both them and their partners comfortable in public places. Tonight, to the eyes of the world, Rick was Calleigh's boyfriend, but Conor had every intention of showing their woman he was just as involved in this experience.

"What did you say to make him laugh so hard?"

Conor grinned against the rim of his glass. "You'll see."

"Conor McGuire, you are full of trouble."

"Aye, but only the best kind. We're havin' a deadly craic, an' I thought you might appreciate a little bard to honor the occasion."

"Me?" Calleigh exclaimed

The players silenced the keys and Conor glanced over at the stage.

"Attention please, everyone! Will Calleigh Wells come up to the stage?"

She stared at Conor, her eyes wide with shock, the silence amplifying the thump-thump-thump of his racing heart. He held out his hand, "Do ye trust me?"

Calleigh glanced over at Rick and out of the corner of his eye, Conor saw him give a slight nod. She slid her hand into his and Conor felt it tremble. He helped her down from the tall bar height table and led her up to the dais. The other patrons parted for them, curious about what was happening, judging by the murmurs that reached his ears as they waited through the crowd. Conor jumped up on stage and turned. Calleigh stood on the floor, her eyes darting around. He could see the anxiety bubbling just beneath the surface, but when their gazes locked, she smiled. Conor nodded to Rick, who stood immediately behind Calleigh. Rick's large hands gripped her waist and lifted her into Conor's waiting arms. He took Calleigh's hand, trying to convey warmth and reassurance, and guided her to the center of the radiant stage. Her cheeks were bright pink, flushed with excitement as the cheers and applause of the audience washed over them. Rick joined them near the piano, and Conor saw him wink at her. He looked over toward the man at the piano and nodded.

"Ladies and gentlemen. We have a unique request this evening. Normally, we would not allow this, but Conor here was very persuasive." He held up the fan of cash in his hand. "Calleigh here is on a date with these two men." He pointed to Rick and Conor.

Conor took a bow as the crowd yelled and wolf whistles floated through the air. He heard a few exclamations of 'you go girl' from a large bridal shower party right by the stage.

"They would like to serenade their sweetheart."

He accepted a microphone for both him and Rick. The intro to *Stay the Night* by Benjamin Orr tinkled from the pianos. The silent seemed to wait with bated breaths in silence. When he and Rick had done this bit years ago, it had been in good fun, but with Calleigh staring at them, he wanted to make sure she understood the lyrics were an echo of their hearts.

Between him and Rick, Conor's voice was the smoother, more captivating of the two. His rich, melodic tone saturated the air, while Rick's gravelly voice added the perfect edge. Conor sang most of the lyrics, his voice rising and falling with the rhythm, while Rick jumped in during the chorus, his energy contagious. They danced around Calleigh, the three of them caught in the electric buzz of the moment, taking turns spinning her and pulling her close. Each touch was electric, the music vibrating in their chests. By the end of the song, excitement and the crowd's growing frenzy flushed their faces. The room had come alive, the entire crowd surging to their feet, roaring for Calleigh to kiss one of them. Conor caught her eye, seeing the brief flash of mischief and resolve before she decided. In a heartbeat, he handed his microphone to Rick, pulling Calleigh into a deep dip as if the world had slowed down around them. He kissed her, his lips claiming hers with a boldness that made the room seem to hold its breath. The applause crashed down like a wave, a roar of approval that shook the stage beneath them. For a heartbeat, the world was just their kiss, soft yet fierce, intense yet playful. Then, with a swift motion, Conor pulled her upright, his arms steady around her, and Rick, grinning, swung her back for his turn. The kiss they shared was passionate, driven by the same fierce energy that had taken over the room. Calleigh tangled her fingers through Rick's hair, pulling him closer, deepening the kiss until the room erupted in whistles and cheers, the sound overwhelming. Conor felt the heat in his chest, the adrenaline pumping through him. Satisfied they'd given the crowd enough of a show, he scooped Calleigh into his arms, her laughter bubbling up like music itself, and made his way toward the exit.

They raced out into the street, the electric buzz of the performance still crackling in the air, and he led them between two buildings. He leaned back against the rough, cool brick, pulling Calleigh into his arms for a deep, passionate kiss that spoke volumes. Their tongues dueled, and his hands grasped her ass to pull their hips together. Rick leaned into their embrace, adding more pressure as their bodies rubbed together. Rick's hands held Calleigh's hips, and each grind of his pelvis pushed her against Conor's erection. Conor felt the sensation as a white-hot brand, burning into his very soul.

Calleigh burned with excitement. Conor's lips devoured hers. One hand massaged her breast while the other tunneled in her hair, pulling on the strands just enough to create extra stimulation. Conor separated their mouths and dropped little kisses down one side of her neck. His hands were at her hips, possessively, and his mouth latched onto her neck, sucking gently at her skin. He nibbled on her ear, his breath hot against her sensitive flesh.

"When we get home, we're going to fuck you all night long. I can't wait to drive my cock deep inside you. Conor has felt the sweet clasp of your body, but now it's my turn. I bet you're dripping for us, aren't you, angel? The thought of us filling you from the front and back excites you, doesn't it? Conor deep inside your ass, while I fill that creamy tight pussy."

She panted as she tried to clench her legs together to ease some of the tension radiating through her.

"I canny wait te feel yer delectable little arse grip me, *muirnín*. You're gonna feel like hot velvet as I fill ye."

She was desperate to get her men inside her as soon as possible. "Home ... Now, before I take you both right here," she growled.

Conor pushed away from the wall. Gripping her hands, the two men raced towards Rick's car, the pounding of their feet on the pavement, a mirror of her heart slamming against her chest as arousal and excitement made her blood rush.

Calleigh knew the trip back to her house should only take twenty minutes, but she felt the time-space continuum was mocking her with its slow passage. Finally, her front door came into view. She exited the vehicle. The night breeze cooled her heated skin. Conor's hand on her back as they walked up the steps, grounded her flighty mind. The soft click as Rick unlocked the door opened her heart to what was about to happen. Silently, they made their way upstairs into her bedroom. Rick lit the candles she kept scattered around to give a little light without turning on the bright overhead. The space was thick with the earthy smell of petrichor, a comforting and intimate aroma that spoke of recent rain. Together, they revealed Calleigh's body to their heated gazes. Conor's aquamarine eyes, intense, and Rick's sapphire eyes, deep and alluring, burned with a shared longing.

Conor picked her up and placed her in the center of the bed, then stepped back. He and Rick stripped. Each unbuttoned their shirts. Chests and firm stomachs showing through the separated edges of fabric. When they removed the material, their muscles flexed, and she caught herself licking her lips. They flicked off their shoes and removed their socks. Hands reached for belts and the closures of their trousers. They were teasing her with the slow strip show. Buttons flicked open, and zippers descended. They stood there without moving. She locked her eyes on their groins, wanting to see those bulges that pressed against the fabric. Her chest heaved, and her eyes burned, but she refused to look away. Finally, they dropped their pants and boxer-briefs and stood in all their nude glory. She moaned. Both were beautifully hard. She raised her eyes to theirs and saw the mirroring burn. Their brief interlude in the kitchen had tantalized Calleigh's appetite. The experience a flash bang of sensation that sated her body, but ultimately only ignited the embers of need in her soul. Tonight, Calleigh would revel in the feast of hedonism and pleasure with the two men who stood before her.

Rick sat on the bed and slid over to lie on his side alongside her. The moment their bare skin made contact for the first time, simultaneous groans escaped from both of them. Rick lifted one of her legs over his hip. Calleigh captured Rick's mouth while wrapping her arms around his neck. She rolled backward when Conor's weight on the bed made the mattress dip. The heat of his hand on her skin as he traced the delicate bumps of her spine had her gasping. He followed every curve and dip of her body until his fingers slide inside her pussy. Firm lips landed on her shoulder and traced a fiery path across her flesh. Reaching up inside her, Conor's long fingers had devastating effects. She felt moisture seeping onto her thighs, and her clit pulsed. His fingers rasped through her folds and rubbed on the swollen tissues. They separated to loosen her for Rick's invasion. Her body throbbed, her soul hungered, her heart echoed the rhythm of those embracing her.

"Conor, yes." She closed her eyes and leaned her head back against him.

"Open your eyes, angel. I want to see that pretty amber darken."

Rick leaned forward and captured her lips, thrusting his tongue into the depths, claiming her. He worked his way down her neck. Sucking and licking across her collarbone. He reached the well of her throat and took a tiny nip. Moving further down, he finally reached her breasts. Swollen and heavy, they ached for his touch or his mouth. He placed little kisses around the edges, moving closer to the tight tips.

She kept trying to guide his mouth to her nipples, but Conor wrapped an arm around her middle and held her still.

She cried out in complaint when his fingers left her body. A second later, she felt the thick coolness of lubrication touch the skin on her backside. Conor's fingers massaged it into the skin around her hole. He pushed at the opening, and she felt the tip of one finger enter. Rick had finally reached the center of her breast, and as though they timed the event, he pulled her nipple into his hot mouth while Conor pushed his finger deep into her ass. She cried out and pushed back against Conor. His other hand reached around her and pinched the nipple, not being worked over by his friend. Rick had moved his hand down and thrust two fingers inside her pussy. Their hands and lips were everywhere. There wasn't a part of her untouched, and it sent her soaring for the skies.

Rick's fingers were working in and out of her pussy, as Conor added a second finger behind her. She felt a pinch and burn but reveled in the both the pressure and fullness. Rick raised his head to once again latch their lips together. His tongue thrust deep, mimicking his fingers below. She felt an orgasm closing in, the edge of the cliff only moments away.

"'Tis gran' *muirnín*. Let go. We'll catch ye."

Suddenly, she jumped, tumbling head over heels into rapturous oblivion. When she landed, Rick had rolled onto his back and lifted her over on top of him. He had her poised over the head of his cock and slowly lowered her down the length. He was a bit wider than Conor, and the pressure was incredible. Even with the foreplay, she felt stretched tight around him.

"Oh God, wait. Too much. I don't—"

"It's okay, angel. We're going to do this slow. I know you can do this. Just breathe for a few seconds. You are so damn tight. Conor was right.

I've never felt anything like you surrounding me." He didn't move any further until her channel softened around him. "There you go, baby. I can feel you loosening up, good girl."

Calleigh rode him slowly. His hands were on her hips, moving her up and down his cock. He filled her to overflowing, but it felt so damn good. He felt different inside her than Conor had. Wider, fuller. His crown was fatter, and it pushed through her burning muscles with tenderness but determination. She could feel herself getting slicker, which made it more comfortable for Rick to move inside her. With a firm but gentle touch, Conor pressed his hand to Calleigh's back, easing her down onto Rick's chest; she felt the steady rhythm of his heartbeat. Rick reached back and opened her round cheeks for Conor's gaze. Calleigh remembered this. The anticipation of what some considered a forbidden touch, but one that never failed to send a surge of excitement through her body, amplifying her pleasure as she begged for more. Conor peppered her neck and back with soft kisses, each one a warm spark against her skin. Then it happened. The pressure against her back entrance, the signal that she willingly submitted every inch of her body to their possession. Conor slowly worked his way in. Calleigh focused on relaxing her muscles. She trusted her men to care for her body as much as her heart.

"*Tá sin ar fheabhas.*"

The soft lyrical tamber of Conor's voice deepened to a raw, throaty growl. He finally made it all the way in, and Calleigh sighed. Her body draped over Rick's while they paused for a moment to let her get used to the sensation. Her mind vacated as she became consumed by the intense physical sensations, craving more of the overwhelming warmth and pressure from her men's bodies.

"Hold on, angel. It's about to get good."

"About to? Any better and I might die."

Rick gave a brief nod, and Calleigh felt Conor withdraw.

"Oh feck' I can feel yer cock rub against mine."

Calleigh felt every inch, too. Only a thin barrier of her body prevented their cocks from thrusting against one another. After a few of Conor's strokes, Rick moved. His hips counter-thrusting into Calleigh's body. Her cries echoed around them as they loved her together.

Calleigh felt so full. Sensations bombarded her. Rick and Conor slid in and out of her body in perfect rhythm. Nothing in her prior experiences prepared her for this. Rick kissed her for long minutes as Conor leaned forward to suck on her neck. All three of them panted. A symphony of labored breathing and moans echoed in the room, each exhale a testament to their journey toward the ultimate moment. The intensity of the emotions being thrown around the room was overwhelming. Both Rick and Conor gasped and whispered love words in her ear. Rick was the first to cry out. His hips bucked up in rapid fire, his hands clenching her hips, and his head thrown back. Conor accelerated, fucking her deeper and harder. Suddenly, all three of them stiffened. Multiple screams rent the air. She felt their cocks pulse as they filled her with their release, and pure mind-blowing ecstasy washed over her. Lights exploded behind her eyes, and she felt as if she were floating.

The feel of a wash cloth wiping between her legs and across her bottom awakened Calleigh. She was lying on her side between the two men. Rick threw the cloth on the floor and lay back down on the bed. Conor rubbed his hands up and down her arms and across her back. He kept placing little kisses on her neck and shoulders. Rick searched her face.

"Are you okay, angel?"

She nodded her head. "It's never been like that before. Thank you."

"For us either, *Ár Ghrá*. Let us rest now, an' we can love some more later."

# Chapter Four

♥

C alleigh rolled over in bed as the sun slanted through the sheers on the windows. As she stretched, she felt a wonderful ache in muscles unused for a long time. Her arms encountered a large hard body, and she turned her head to see Conor still asleep next to her. Rolling to her side, she watched him in slumber. His auburn hair looked more red in the sunlight. His fair skin showed traces of morning beard, and she wondered what it would feel like rubbing against her skin. She reached up to trace the slash of his eyebrows and ran a fingertip across his lips. She gasped as he opened his mouth and sucked her finger inside. The pull made her womb flutter, and she looked up to see those blue-green eyes twinkling in amusement. Pulling her finger out of his mouth, she leaned forward to kiss him.

"Morning."

"Mornin' *muirnín*." He reached out and pulled Calleigh against him.

Since Kevin had died, waking up with a man in her bed had become unfamiliar, but with Conor it felt right. The only person missing was Rick. She had missed the closeness and lethargy of waking with a lover after a night of passion. She burrowed deeper in the blankets and snuggled in closer to the warmth of Conor's body, tangling their legs beneath the sheets. His eyes had closed again, and he caressed her hair as she laid her head on his chest.

"Conor?"

"Hmm?"

"What are you saying when you speak Gaelic? Not everything, but I'd like to know a couple of words."

He rolled to his back and took Calleigh with him to lie on top of him. She propped her chin on her hands and looked up at him. "*Muirnín* means sweetheart or beloved." He kissed her forehead. "*Mo ghrá* means my love." He tucked a loose strand of hair behind her ear. "*Ár ghrá* means *our* love." He frowned. "Does it bother you when I speak the language of Shannon? That ye canny understand? I'll stop. Sometimes 'tis not something I do on purpose, it just comes out."

"No. It doesn't bother me. It's a beautiful language and sounds so damn sexy when your deep voice whispers in my ear. I was just curious."

"Usually the unconscious stuff only happens if I'm troilled, really full aff, or when you've melted me brain with hedonism." He reached under her arms and lifted her up so he could kiss her.

Conor's lips were soft with morning sleepiness. His tongue slipped inside and lazily rubbed against hers. The soft licks were just as devastating as the more demanding, intense kisses. Her insides were turning to liquid as she floated in dreamy desire. Suddenly, her world spun as Conor rolled. She landed on her back, and he levered himself over her. Her legs automatically separated to cradle his hips. The kiss deepened. Conor's hands threaded through her hair and held their lips together. His pelvis thrust against her center, and she tilted her hips. She felt the moisture gathering between her legs and raised her legs to wrap around his back. One push and Conor was inside her. The invasion was heavenly. She cried out into his mouth. There was no pausing this time. He plunged deep in rhythmic strokes, hips canting forward and back as she lifted into the thrusts.

Conor separated from Calleigh's sweet lips. The feel of her warm wet channel clasping him was heaven. She was laid out for him like a feast, and he wanted to gorge himself on every delectable inch of her skin. He braced himself on his forearms and dipped his head to her full, soft breasts. He traced his tongue over the thin line of a blue vein. Encircling the areola, he put the turgid plush nipple into his mouth and suckled.

The boys had nursed here. Someday, his child would nurse here. He wanted to see that. A small head nestled to her chest, the scent of baby powder in the air. A child created in love by the three of them. It wouldn't matter if he or Rick were the biological father. They had known and accepted that when they'd decided they wanted to embrace this lifestyle permanently.

He increased the pace of his thrusts. Calleigh's muscles were rippling down the length of his cock. He was so damn hard he knew this wouldn't last long, but was determined to give her the best orgasm possible. She gripped him, her legs wrapped around his back and her heels pressed into his rear. Her hips lifted into each one of his thrusts. He reached up and snatched a pillow from the top of the bed. A quick move and Conor placed the pillow beneath Calleigh's hips. He pushed her legs apart and sampled her honey. Calleigh's moans were almost as sweet as juices that slickened her lips.

"Conor. Oh God, please."

As tasty as his love was, Conor's cock throbbed with the need to once again be embraced by her velvety channel. He gripped the base of his cock and poised the head at her opening. He pushed just the tip inside, closing his eyes to savor the clasp of her tight, hot flesh. Conor braced his hands on either side of her torso. Calleigh opened her eyes slowly. He stared into her gaze, enraptured by how their natural amber color had darkened. He counted her breaths and only when his body shook did he drive his hips downward. The change in angle allowed him to reach the deepest parts of her. Calleigh's high-pitched cry, signaled her delight in the new position.

"I love being inside ye, *muirnín*. Yer made fer Rick and I te love. Yer body an' heart belong te us now." He groaned above her. "I have held back fer the past year, but no more. I canny keep me hands aff ye any longer."

"I want you, Conor. I want to feel you touch me. I want to feel Rick touch me. I need you both so much. I'd forgotten how it feels to be loved, but I've never been loved as I have by the two of you ... Harder Conor... Please ... Please... I need all of you. Don't hold back."

He looked down to see Calleigh's eyes wide open. The black of her pupils nearly occluding the rich amber color. Her words sent fire screaming through his body. Lust and love raged inside him. He lifted her legs over his shoulders and braced one arm beside her head. He fucked her unmercifully as she asked. Stroking faster, harder and deeper into her welcoming body. She panted, little cries and moans escaping from her throat in time to his thrusts. Their eyes locked, her entire body trembled and her cry echoed around the room. Sharp contractions squeezed around him—oh God! He came and came and came from the very depths of his soul as she milked him dry.

Conor rolled to his side. They were both breathing hard, and his pulse was racing. This was the first time she had been with just one of them. As much as he loved sharing Calleigh with Rick and devastating her senses with their combined passion, this morning felt special between the two of them. As if they'd cemented their bond as a couple outside what the three of them had shared the night before. He heard footsteps at the door and looked up to see Rick enter the room. He stepped up to the side of the bed and bent over to kiss Calleigh.

"Good morning, angel. Conor gives electrifying wake up calls, doesn't he?"

"Are you upset we did that without you? It didn't occur to me you might be jealous about me having sex with Conor while you aren't here."

"No, baby. I'm incredibly turned on, but never upset. You'll have private time with Conor, just as the two of us will have time together." He sat down next to her and smoothed back her hair that had flown all over the place with their exertions. "We love sharing you, but more importantly, we love you individually. It's only natural for you to want to spend time with Conor apart from me, and spend time with me apart from him. That's one thing that will naturally develop between the three of us. Now, how about we all go downstairs and get some breakfast? You lazy bones have slept the morning away."

She smiled and Conor leaned over to kiss her cheek. Rick stood and reached a hand down to help Calleigh out of bed. When she placed her hand in his, he pulled hard and, dipping his shoulder into her stomach, lifted her over his shoulder. She squealed, and he slapped her on the ass. Conor didn't bother to hold in the bark of laughter at her indignant cry.

"Put me down, you Neanderthal," she said, laughing.

"Never. I've hunted and gathered all morning to provide food for my woman. Now, I will carry you to my cave."

"But I'm naked!" she yelled as Rick walked out the door and headed for the stairs.

Conor heard Rick ask why that was a problem as his footsteps descended the staircase. He looked over to the seat by the window and saw that Rick had brought up his jeans from the car. They had packed a change of clothes, anticipating a sleepover. He slipped them on, foregoing a shirt for the moment. He picked up Calleigh's robe from the same chair and followed the pair down into the kitchen.

Rick carried Calleigh into the kitchen and perched her on the countertop. She wrapped her legs around his hips and locked her arms around his back. He couldn't look away from the bright glow of happiness in her eyes. He'd never been privileged to see her all flushed and rumpled in the morning and wanted to enjoy the view. Her hair was a cloud of honey blonde around her shoulders, her lips swollen and moist from Conor's kisses. Her nipples, already tight, begged for his touch, and he saw evidence of her and Conor's loving on her pussy lips and thighs.

"You are so beautiful," he said reverently.

He craved another taste of her and reached around the back of her neck to pull her into a kiss. The first touch of their lips was soft, but not hesitant. He opened his lips and flicked his tongue out, a fleeting touch to her upper lip. The edges of their lips brushed for several counts, breathing softly into each other's mouths. He prolonged the anticipation, letting it build inside them. Waiting for that moment when they felt as if they'd explode if they didn't get the touch they craved. Finally, he couldn't take it any longer, and he bent to her and locked their lips together. His tongue plunged into her mouth, no longer soft and teasing. He wanted to consume Calleigh's essence. Her kiss grabbed something inside him, and he dragged her closer, his hands threaded through that soft halo of hair holding her in place. He groaned as her tongue twisted with his. When they finally lifted their heads, he looked over to the doorway and saw Conor watching them. He was holding out Calleigh's robe. Rick lifted her off the countertop so she could walk over, and Conor assisted her into the thin, silky covering, which to his satisfaction conformed to each of her lush curves.

They were sitting at the table when the front door opened, and the thundering of little feet echoed through the house and two little voices called out for mommy in stereo. Rick looked up at Conor and Calleigh. He hadn't been expecting the boys to see them in their morning dishevel. Conor had a slight deer in the headlight look about him, but Calleigh seemed calm as a cucumber. He went with the flow.

A little body was barreling toward him when he snaked out an arm, caught the energized bundle, and lifted it onto his lap. He looked and figured out that he had Brandon.

"What's up, speedy?"

"Hi Wick. Why you hewa?"

"We stayed with your mommy last night. Did you munchkins have breakfast at grandma's?"

"Uh-huh. We have teareos."

Brandon was playing with his bare chest. The little boy had probably never seen a grown man without his shirt. His little fingers twisted in Rick's chest hair. Granted, he didn't have much, but it still stung. He lifted the small hands, blew a raspberry on the palms, the tickle eliciting unrestrained, joyful giggles.

"Where you shoot? Why you have hair?" Brandon was pointing at his chest.

"My shirt is upstairs, and I have hair because I'm an adult. When you grow up you'll look like me."

He looked up to see Mikey in Conor's arms, having a similar conversation. Calleigh was eating her breakfast with a smile on her face. Brandon wiggled, wanting off his lap, so Rick set him down and he ran over to Calleigh to give her a hug. Mikey did the same, then came over to him.

He lifted Mikey up onto his lap. "Did you have fun at grandma's last night?"

"Uh-huh. We play game."

"You did? What game did you play?"

"Hide and seek. We win."

Mikey had a huge smile on his face and bounced on his lap in excitement. Rick raised his hand to give Mikey a high-five. They had taught the boys that little game not too long ago, and they got a kick out of it.

"They most certainly did. Mikey and Brandon are very creative hiders. You better watch out, Calleigh. They might be better than you were at their age."

Rick turned his head when Calleigh's mom entered the kitchen. "Good morning, Lilly."

She raised an eyebrow at the state of undress present in the kitchen. "Morning Rick, Conor. Did the three of you have fun last night?"

"Yes, thank you for watching the boys. We wanted to treat Calleigh to a night out on the town."

"Then I'm glad you all had fun. Calleigh, dear, can I speak to you for a moment?" She turned and walked out to the living room.

Calleigh rolled her eyes, and Rick smiled. "Do you mind?" She asked, gesturing to the deadly duo.

"You never have to ask, angel."

Calleigh stood. The time had come to face the music with her mother. Calleigh knew that while discussing sexuality with a parent was always difficult, she was fortunate because her mother already supported friends who lived outside hetero-normative relationships. When she entered the living room, her mom was sitting in the large chair by the bow windows.

"Yes?"

"Calleigh, is there something you want to tell me?"

She saw her mom's eyes twinkle and a little smug smile on her lips. Calleigh huffed and rolled her eyes back at her. "Don't act so obtuse. I think it's fairly obvious. Are you going to give us any trouble?"

She frowned. "Honey, don't get defensive. I just want you and the boys to be happy and healthy. The three of you have had enough heartache for this lifetime. If this is what you all want, then your father and I will support you. Plus, I've seen the sparks flying around this house for the past year from all sides. Yours may have been a little more subtle, but still there. I know those men love you, and God knows, they adore Michael and Brandon. I'm glad you're ready for a new relationship. Should I bother asking if it's only one of them or both?" She smiled.

Calleigh threw her hands up in the air. "Oh for Pete's sake, mom. Fine." She started pacing around the living room. "Conor, Rick, and I have taken our relationship to the next level. You can call us a unit or throuple or whatever. We want to have a marriage of three, eventually." She stopped and looked over at her mother, who sat calmly in the chair. "Their words, not mine."

"Are you sure you know what you're getting yourself into?"

"Does anyone when they start a new relationship? If you're asking whether I'm comfortable being with both of them, the answer is yes. I love them. They have been my best friends, and now, they're my lovers. And since you are being so nosy, you may as well know that not all aspects of this relationship are foreign to me." She let that sink in and saw the moment her mom comprehended her meaning. "I can see you understand."

Lilly leaned forward in the chair. "You and Kevin?"

Calleigh sat on the sofa, making sure her robe stayed closed. "Yes, occasionally. Back in college. So you see, I know this type of situation would not shock or disgust him were he still here."

Lilly stood and joined her daughter on the sofa. She turned her body to face Calleigh. "Have you thought about how Kevin's mom will react when she finds out? It may be more of a shock to her than to me and your father. We're neither naïve nor averse to alternative lifestyles, but she is much more conservative."

"I know that, but she really only sees the boys once or twice a year. It may take some getting used to, but I don't think she would let it affect her relationship with Kevin's children." She reached over and gave her mom a hug. "Thanks, mom. I love you."

"I love you, too, sweetie. Now why don't I go gather up the boys and get some toys out, and you and your men can go upstairs and finishing dressing. Although I must say, I greatly appreciated the view when I walked into the kitchen earlier."

"Mother!"

She patted Calleigh's cheek. "I'm happily married, dear, not dead."

# Chapter Five

♥

"Hey Calleigh!"

She looked up when the doors to the operating room opened and Miranda Burns walked in. She rushed over and hugged her friend.

"Hi, I didn't know you were on this case."

"I may have pulled some strings and traded cases with another first assistant when I saw they assigned you to Chase's procedure."

"A benefit of being married to the surgeon?"

"Maybe. It's been too long since we had a tete-a-tete."

"I agree. Even though this isn't exactly a coffee shop where we can sip lattes and gossip. Any minute now, a four-month-old little girl is being wheeled in. You and your husband are going to be focused on the strip craniectomy, and I need to make sure the angel only has sweet dreams throughout the entire procedure."

"True, but I know Chase has complete faith in you and it's nice having a friend in the OR. Makes the extensive surgeries ... I don't know, not as stressful in a way?"

"I hear you. Sharing your work space with like-minded people makes the hours pass easier. It's going to be a long one today too, because right after this I have a spinal fusion for severe scoliosis with Dr. Hayre. He's a fantastic surgeon, but not exactly an ambassador for collaboration."

Miranda winced. "Yikes. I hate surgeries with Hayre. And that's like a seven-hour procedure, right?"

"Yeah, but at least I have a three-day weekend coming up. The boys are off school and I took PTO. Been trying to decide what we should do for the day."

"Oh, my God. I'm off too. Let's take the kids out!"

"That would be fun. We could go to the zoo or the aquarium or..."

"The Children's Museum," they said simultaneously.

"I can get us discount passes from the library and we can have lunch down by the harbor."

"That sounds fantastic. Gabby would love to see Mikey and Brandon again. She looks up to them so much."

"And they love her too. God, it's hard to believe she's two already."

Miranda laughed. "Tell me about it. Seems like just yesterday we were standing in my bedroom and you waddled out to announce your water had broken."

Miranda and Chase, along with their husband Vic, had been so supportive when Mikey and Bran were born during Kevin's deployment. Miranda had even been Calleigh's birth coach in the delivery room. Then, after Kevin's death, the threesome checked in with her almost daily. Sometimes to lend a helping hand, other times just to be an ear for her grief. As Calleigh developed her friendship with Rick and Conor, she didn't call on Miranda, Chase, and Vic as much, but when their daughter Gabriella was born Calleigh tried to payback all the love and parental support the family had shown her. The little angel was so sweet, and occasionally made Calleigh ache for a girl of her own, but then most days it took everything in her to keep her head above water with the twins.

"Then, just a few months later, Gabby graced the world with her presence."

"Yes, with all the fanfare of royalty. And the little princess has her fathers' complete devotion ever since."

"Speaking of little girls, here comes our patient."

Calleigh checked the backpack to make sure she had all the kid paraphernalia necessary for a day out. It actually felt strange to spend the morning at home versus getting the boys packed up for before school care while it was still dark. Usually, Calleigh only took time off if one of the boys came down with a virus or had pediatrician appointments. And she always felt guilty for leaving the other staff short handed. When Calleigh put in her request for this vacation day three months ago, her supervisor had immediately texted her to ask what if she was planning a day of self indulgence. Calleigh had laughed and said she was lucky these days if she got to use the bathroom in private, let alone spend an entire day pampering herself.

"Mikey! Brandon! It's time to go."

They actually had another fifteen minutes before they needed to leave to meet the Burns family, but it usually took that long just to get out the door, so Calleigh always built in a buffer. She checked the backpack for a third time.

"Two changes of clothes, extra underwear, snacks, juice boxes, baby wipes, hand sanitizer, band-aids, lip balm—"

"Mommy! Can Luna come with us?"

"She can come in the car but not to the museum. We wouldn't want her to get lost."

"What about Rexotron?"

"Same!"

Luna and Rexotron were the current favorite toys. The stuffed lion cub was rarely out of Mikey's sight, and Brandon's robotic dinosaur loved to swoop in and capture other poor defenseless toys.

"But Evan say Daniel the Tiger is there, and I want Luna to meet him!"

Calleigh set the backpack down by the front door and walked back toward the playroom. She would not yell through the house. "Mikey, we talked about this last night at bedtime. We want Luna to stay safe and come home, right?"

Mikey nodded and hugged his lion cub.

"You take such good care of her, and the last thing I want is for another child to accidentally hurt her because they are playing too rough. And what if she got lost? I want us all to have a fantastic day exploring, and I'm afraid Luna might get set down somewhere in all the excitement. That's why she's going to guard the car for us while we are out with Gabriella and Miranda."

"But what if she gets hungry?"

"We will leave her and Rexotron snacks."

"Rexotron will make Luna his snack!" Brandon said while making the toy fly right toward the stuffed lion.

"Brandon Wells!"

Her youngest froze and looked at her over his shoulder. "Yes?"

Calleigh gave Brandon her best mom stare.

"Sorry, Luna. I promise not to eat you ... today." Brandon made the dinosaur say in a growly voice.

Calleigh was taking the win for the moment. "Okay, you two head to the hallway and get your shoes from the parking spot."

The pair ran down the hall, and she looked around the playroom. It was a disaster as usual and her fingers itched to pick up the debris, but it wasn't worth the effort at the moment. Tonight she'd get the deadly duo to help her. Which usually meant she, Rick, or Conor did most of the work, but the intent was to teach the boys how to clean up after themselves and care for their toys. Some days, lessons resonated more than others.

When she got back to the front door, both boys sat on the floor near the coat closet. They each had tried to put on their shoes, but things went slightly awry. "Good job, boys, but I think we need to fix just two things. Do you know what they are?"

"No." Mikey said.

Calleigh squatted down and lifted her sons feet up for inspection. "Do your two shoes look the same?"

"Nu-huh, but I like dat way."

"Hmm, and what about you Bran? Do your shoes match?"

"Nope."

She looked back and forth. "So, should we make our shoes match?"

"No!"

"Okay. How about this, you can wear one of each kind—"

"Yay!"

"But you both have to wear one right and one left shoe. Otherwise you'll walk in circles all day!"

She spent a couple of minutes getting shoegate settled and grabbed their lightweight jackets. The weather was nice for October, but they all still needed some outerwear. Especially since they were going to be down near the harbor. Fifteen minutes later, she buckled her troops into their car seats.

Getting to the museum would take about twenty minutes. Calleigh had thought about taking the T since they lived close to the red line and the museum was a short walk from the south station, but she'd found that the charge to park was worth her sanity when they had adventure days. That way, if the shit hit the fan, they could always bail and get back home without having to navigate the MBTA system. Had Rick and Conor been with her, then they could always divide and conquer, but a solo expedition required some sacrificial usage of fossil fuels.

"Now, I want you boys to remember that Gabriella is smaller than you. You need to set big boy examples of how to behave politely."

"But she a girl. Girls are gwoss."

"Michael, that's not nice. Besides, you have friends at school who are girls. What about Paige?"

"Paige likes to play with boys. Gabby is..."

"Is what?"

"Mommy, I not try to be mean, but she's ... she's just a lot."

Calleigh snorted. Brandon's little ears had picked up that phrase from some unsuspecting adult conversation. Ever since the boys turned three, the three of them had some of the most interesting car conversations. Their vocabulary seemed to expand daily, for better and for worse. It was fascinating to learn how they viewed the world and their place in it.

"I get it. Girls are different from boys. But you love and play with me and I'm a girl."

"You ouwa mommy. That's diffwent."

"Fair. But I still expect the two of you to play nice with Gabby and any other children at the museum today."

"Okey donkey!"

She glanced at her two sweet little hellions in the rearview mirror. Ever since they turned their car seats to forward facing, it was much easier to keep an eye on them. God, they were getting big. How was it that the last three years felt interminable but flashed by her at the speed of light at the same time? Calleigh made the turn off Seaport Boulevard onto Sleeper Street. There was a garage on Farnsworth where she might grab a spot if the Boston parking gods were in her favor. A couple of turns and a quick prayer later, she peaked at the entry.

"Yes! We're in luck, boys."

"Yay! Why are we wucky?"

"Because Mommy found us a parking spot only two blocks from the museum. That means no stroller."

"Good. We big boys now. Only babies wike Gabby use stowers."

Calleigh found an empty spot. When she, Rick, and Conor planned whole days out, they still brought the double stroller. Even though the boys boasted they didn't need the wheels, their small bodies always slumped with weary. The last thing they wanted at the end of a great day was a total meltdown because of exhaustion.

Once she secured the backpack and strapped Luna and Rexotron into the car seats, the three of them stepped out of the garage. The cool morning air hit them as they made their way to the museum. They made it to Congress, where Calleigh paused to let the boys gawk in the windows of the Boston Fire Museum. Both Mikey and

Brandon had visited before with Rick and Conor on a boy's day out over the summer. Normally Calleigh would let them linger, but she knew Miranda and Gabby were waiting.

"Come on boys, adventure awaits!" The entrance to the children's museum was on the harbor side, so Calleigh had to keep her troops marching. "Whoever gives me two examples of things plants need to grow gets to pick the first activity."

"That easy, mommy. water and sun."

As they passed a Dunkin', Calleigh almost moaned. She needed a hit of caffeine. "Great job, Mikey. Okay Bran, tell me what happens when you mix water and soil?"

"Mud Pies! There Mommy, look, I see it! There's the giant milk bottle."

"I see it bubby. We're almost there." As soon as they passed the edge of the brick building, Calleigh saw Miranda and Gabby waiting for them on the harbor walk. "Oh look, one of Gabby's daddies came too." Chase stood with his hands braced on the crossbar of the stroller that, for the moment, contained his daughter. "Hey guys! Sorry, we walked from the garage."

"No problem. Hi Mikey. Hi Bran. Are you ready for an awesome day?"

"Let's do this!" Mikey cheered.

Two tiny generals hauled Calleigh toward the entrance, much to Miranda and Chase's amusement. They scanned their passes and a sea of humanity instantly surrounded them. It seemed most of Bostonian parents had the same idea for the day. Straight ahead of them was a two story climbing netted structure that gave Calleigh heart palpitations. She caught Miranda and Chase's gaze and nodded toward the science playground. Chase, being the genius he was, did a fantastic job of picking up on her cues and got the boys to chase him into the bubble room. Miranda let Gabriella out of her stroller so she could join the group near a trough to splash and play in the soapy water.

"It's so great to see you." Calleigh said.

Miranda laughed. "You saw me just the other day."

"Yes, but you know what I mean."

Miranda put her arm around Calleigh. "I do. And I'm glad to see you too."

They watched as Chase and the kids all competed to see who could blow the biggest bubble.

"He's so good with them."

Miranda smiled. "Yeah. He's really taken to fatherhood. Vic too, just differently."

Calleigh smiled and bumped shoulders with Miranda. "Chase is the fun parent, isn't he?"

Miranda rolled her eyes. "Totally. But Vic is the one she goes to when she wants quiet time and hugs."

"I guess that's one thing about being both mom and dad. I've had to be all the parents, all the time."

"And you've done an amazing job. I know Rick and Conor have helped, but they're not really Mikey and Bran's dads."

Calleigh smiled. "Well ... that's kind of evolving."

"Oh?"

Calleigh, smiling, trailed the group out of the bubble room as the boys departed. They went across the hall to the raceway exhibit. She looked over her shoulder at Miranda and winked.

"Calleigh Wells, you better dish out the goods right this instant!"

She picked up a silver sphere and set it at the top of the track, then let it go. The ball gathered speed as it rolled down the track, then soared into the air at the end. Like the ball, her heart raced down the path toward this new relationship with Rick and Conor, the excitement both exhilarating and terrifying. She hoped she'd land and not crash and burn at the end of her track.

Mikey and Bran were busy adding balls to the spiral tower while Chase and Gabby were at the far end of the room with the golf ball tube wall.

"So we might have ... stopped fighting our urges?"

"I didn't realize there were ... urges."

Calleigh bit her lower lip. "For a while. On all our sides. But it wasn't until recently that I even considered dating again."

"This is a good thing. I know the boys love Rick and Conor, so it's not like you have to introduce them to a stranger. You three can take things slow and feel out how a relationship between you all might work. And if you need any tips on how to make things hot, I'm just a text away."

Calleigh laughed. "Oh, that part we figured out real quick."

"You saucy mix!"

Chase looked back at them, hearing his wife's exclamation, and winked at Miranda. Her friend blew him a kiss. Calleigh whipped out her phone to take a picture of the boys and posted it to her, Rick, and Conor's group chat. A pair of heart emojis appeared on the screen within seconds. It wouldn't surprise her if, by the end of the day, one or both of her men ditched work early and joined their merry band of misfits.

# Chapter Six

C alleigh was bone tired. She'd taken a double shift at the hospital because one of the other nurses had called in sick. Fortunately, she didn't have to worry about calling her mom to come watch the boys anymore. A month ago, Rick and Conor sublet their condo and moved in. Calleigh had been slightly worried they were moving too fast, but honestly on nights, or well she guessed mornings, like this, it was a godsend having them at home.

She reached into her locker to grab her purse and coat. A nor'easter had arrived yesterday, and the temperatures were near record lows and predicted to stay that way for the next several days. November had returned. Hard to believe, but true. She sat on the bench beside the lockers as tears pooled in her eyes. Kevin's death anniversary approached, always a tough day. Kevin's mom was coming to visit once again, and Calleigh supposed she needed to prepare for questions. However, she didn't want her relationship with Rick and Conor to take center stage. The day was about honoring Kevin's memory, and sharing stories with the boys about their father. They always went and visited Kevin as a family. They'd laid him to rest in Massachusetts National Cemetery. Calleigh would like it if Rick and Conor came with them this year, but had yet to ask them.

Tracking the changes in her life over the last five years would give her whiplash if she thought about them all at once. She'd gone from single college student to married. Then, six months into her and Kevin's marriage, her husband deployed. Calleigh's daily life reverted to the existence of an independent woman for the year. Sometimes she got lonely, but she'd never been one who craved a boisterous social life, so an occasional dinner out with friends satisfied her with Kevin gone. She'd finished her master's degree and got a job at New England Baptist. Kevin returned from overseas, and they spent lots of time renewing their connection. When her doctor confirmed her pregnancy, both she and Kevin were stunned. However, once the shock wore off, they reveled in the prospect of starting a family. They planned on him retiring from the reserves and staying home with the baby for the first few months. However, when they told Kevin about his deployment right as she crossed over the first trimester, he postponed his retirement. Coincidently, just two weeks after she started her dream job at Mass General. She supported her husband's choice to join the service, but she would be lying if she said she hadn't spent a few evenings panicking about diving into motherhood alone.

Now Calleigh's house had never been so busy or filled with love. The boys thrived on having Rick and Conor around, and so far, didn't even seem to question their presence in the house every day. They questioned everything else around them but seem to accept Rick and Conor's presence with no problem. All her men had formed a boys' only club, which she found hilarious. Every night, Rick or Conor would take them upstairs for baths, then both men would read a story before bedtime. When club time was over, she would come in and say goodnight. Rick and Conor's willingness to immerse themselves in fatherhood was amazing. Not to mention a perk on her end. Sleeping in their arms was heavenly, and the sex was beyond anything she could have imagined. Their time together, whether collectively or individually, always generated tremendous passion, surpassing all previous encounters.

"Calleigh? You okay, hon?"

She jumped at the voice. "Jeez, Carla, you scared me. Sorry, I was drifting. Just finished a double, and my mind wandered."

Carla smiled. "I know that feeling. Do you need a lift home? You usually take the T, don't you?"

"Normally, yes, but Rick is picking me up this morning."

"Good, I'm glad you won't be by yourself, walking around half asleep. Well, I'm off. Gotta get the kids to school."

Calleigh waved goodbye as Carla ran out of the locker room. She had introduced Conor and Rick to Carla and her husband a couple of weeks before. The couple had barely even blinked when Calleigh introduced Rick and Conor as her boyfriends. This had given her the courage to be open about their relationship to a couple of other choice colleagues. Most had reacted positively. One nurse had pulled Calleigh aside and read her the riot act, saying she should keep private business private. That the hospital was a place of business, and treating coworkers as confidants and friends only lead to repercussions in the workplace. On one hand, Calleigh understood the woman's concern, but she couldn't spend twelve hours a day with her team and treat them as only polite strangers. It wasn't as if she posted a flyer in the breakroom divulging her private business. If people spread gossip about her relationship, then that was on them. She wasn't embarrassed, and she wasn't the only hospital employee who dared to be true to themselves.

She glanced at the clock; it read 7:15 a.m. Rick would be there soon, so she closed up her locker and headed for the entry doors.

She groaned as she stood inside the doors and saw Miles walking toward her from the parking lot. The man had been making a nuisance of himself since that one date they'd had almost two months ago. It seemed as if he were always the person she had to talk to in radiology no matter what time of day, and he always tried to drag out their conversation. Every time they passed in the hall, he would touch her. Nothing threatening, but always annoying. A hand on a shoulder or he would even grab her hand and clasp it when she tried to pull back. He always seemed to be in the cafeteria at the same time as Calleigh, and he frequently would stand at the employee's entrance and walk with her to the T, even though he lived on the other side of town.

She had said nothing to Conor or Rick because she knew how protective they were, and they really, really hated Miles. It was almost funny. The mention of his name would elicit scowls from them, and she'd hear them mutter "wanker" and "gobshite" under their breath. Maybe she'd talk to Vic since Miles reported to him. Well, technically, since Vic was director of the musculoskeletal imaging and intervention, Miles' supervisor reported to Vic. Maybe she could use her friendship with Vic to handle this nuisance in house.

Miles was almost to the doors now, and Calleigh turned her back, trying to be less noticeable. Unfortunately, it didn't work.

"Hey Cal! I thought you were off today."

She reluctantly turned around to face him. "I am. I just came off a double."

"Oh wow, you must be beat. Can I give you a lift? I don't start for another half hour, and was just planning on getting a cup of coffee. Do you want to grab one with me?"

She saw Rick's car pull into the parking lot and breathed a sigh of relief. "No, thank you, Miles. My boyfriend just pulled in. He's taking me home."

Miles moved with such speed that she wasn't prepared. Grabbing her upper arm and squeezing, he pushed her back against the wall.

"What the hell do you think you're doing? Let go of me!"

"What do you mean 'boyfriend'? What about us?"

"Let go, you're hurting me, Miles." She tried to wrench her arm away from his grasp, but he held tighter, and she winced. "There *is* no us, Miles. We went on one date two months ago."

"We had chemistry, Cal. You can't deny it. I know you felt it when I kissed you." He loosened his grip on her arm and reached up to caress the side of her face.

Calleigh turned her head away from his touch, but his fingers clasped her chin, and he turned it back.

"All I remember feeling was apathy."

"Apathy, huh? Well, maybe, I ought to remind how good it was between us."

Miles was holding her head in a tight grip, and she watched him angle for another kiss, but when his lips were about to touch, a large arm wrapped around his neck.

"I wouldn't do that if I were you. Let go of her. Now!"

She looked up to see Rick. He was furious, the sapphires of his eyes glowing.

Miles' hand released her head, and she angled away from the wall to stand beside Rick.

Rick let go of Miles and gave him a little push so his back was to the wall. "Just what in the hell did you think you were doing? Is that the way you treat women?"

"Who the hell are you? This is none of your business. I was trying to have a private moment with my girl here."

Rick snorted. "I know for a fact that she is in no way, shape, or form *your girl*. In fact, I can guarantee that she's *my girl*. I know this because I live with her."

Miles looked over at Calleigh. "You slut! You go from being the ice queen of the hospital to shacking up with some guy in two months?"

Calleigh was pissed. How dare this little twerp first accost her and then turn belligerent when she turned him down? She was so glad in retrospect that she hadn't continued to date Miles. She had no need for a Jekyll and Hyde character in her or the boys' lives.

"Actually, I'm living with two men. Rick here and Conor whom I'm sure would love the honor of meeting you. The two of them are worth more to me than any number of you. Stay away from me, Miles. Stop calling my department, stop accidentally running into me in the hallways and stop hanging around the doors when I leave. I have no problem alerting the administration if you harass me any further after today. Oh, and I'll be sure to mention your harassment to Dr. Burns. He's a good friend of ours."

"You try it and I'll call Social Services. I bet they would love to know that a single woman is fucking two different men in the same house as her young, impressionable sons. You never know, if they're both fucking you, maybe they're even fucking each other. I'm a conscientious citizen. It would only be right for me to alert them that young children are living with sexual deviants."

A couple of people, either coming on shift or leaving, were standing there watching the scene. She didn't want to perpetuate anything further, so she turned her back and walked out to Rick's waiting car.

They sat in silence as Rick drove down Commonwealth Avenue. Calleigh saw his knuckles were white from gripping the steering wheel so hard. She couldn't tell if he was mad at her or the situation, so she figured it would be best to wait until he started the inevitable conversation. Silence reigned as they pulled up to the house. Rick turned off the ignition but remained in the driver's seat.

He took a deep breath and let it out. "Let's go inside. Conor called Lilly, and she's coming to pick up Mike and Brandon so you can get some sleep. Before you argue, she volunteered to pick them up last night, but we told her the boys would stay with us overnight and she could have them today. Then you, me and Conor can sit down and talk. I didn't want to start any discussion of this nature without him."

She nodded her head and climbed out of the car. As she reached the front door, she noticed her hand shaking a little as she reached for the handle. Rick must have seen it too, because he put his hand on top of hers and gave it a little squeeze. The trembling stopped. One of their small touches transformed everything.

She opened the door and walked inside.

Rick was beyond incensed. He'd seen red when he'd spotted that Miles character holding Calleigh to the wall and trying to force himself on her. The sliding glass doors almost hadn't opened fast enough as he'd raced towards them. When his arm had locked around that son-of-a-bitch's throat, he'd wanted to squeeze the life out of him.

These intense reactions were not normal for him, and it made him feel very off balanced.

From what Calleigh had mentioned, it sounded as if this guy had been bothering her since their date months ago. Rick didn't understand why she would keep something like that from him and Conor. Protecting her was their duty. He had taken a vow. And those things Miles had said at the end just made it worse. But to threaten Calleigh like that was inexcusable.

Rick had used the drive home to calm his emotions a little so he wouldn't fly off the handle when they sat down as a family to talk about it. Seeing Calleigh's hand shake as she'd reached for the knob had sent a knife through his heart. He was mad, wanted to be mad, but he did not want Calleigh to fear that he would take his anger out on her. After they had their talk, he would feed her some breakfast, then put her to bed. He knew she had to be exhausted, and having to deal with this crap after working a double shift was not good for her.

It was Saturday, and normally he and Conor wouldn't have to work, but they had a major project deadline approaching. The two of them had promised to put in some extra hours, but that was before he'd witnessed the scene at the hospital. He stepped into the kitchen to text his boss that they wouldn't make it to the office after all, citing a family emergency. His boss knew their living situation and didn't question if he and Conor would make up the hours later that week. When he walked back into the living room, Conor was walking down the hallway, tucking in his shirt. He looked up and stopped in the middle of the treads.

"What's wrong?"

"I text Craig. We're not going in today. We need to have a family discussion."

Vic stopped in front of Rick. "Where's Calleigh? What happened?"

"That SOB Miles has been hassling her at the hospital. When I pulled up, he had her fucking pinned to the wall and was trying to kiss her." He spun around and started pacing in the living room. "The little fucker even threatened to call Social Services on her for living with us."

"I'm gonna kill that feckin' little gobshite! Where's *Ár ghrá*? Is she gran'?"

"She's fine. She's saying good morning to the boys before Lilly comes to pick them up." He smiled when he remembered how Calleigh had stood up to the little fucker before they'd left.

"What are ye smilin' fer?"

"Calleigh gave no quarter. Once I got her free of his clutches, she lit into him. Our sweetheart has gumption, if not the physical strength to defend herself."

"Bleedin' mess. If he had hurt her..."

"I know ... I know."

Rick heard footsteps on the stairs and saw Calleigh come down, with Mike and Brandon in tow. Both boys had rather hangdog expressions on their faces. He schooled his features so the boys wouldn't see any distress. Conor walked over and squatted at eye level.

"Are ye *gasurs* ready for a day with *mamó*?" They both shook their heads.

"We want mommy," Brandon said.

"I know, *mo greine*. Your ma had te work all night, and she's real knackered. She's goin' te take a nap, and when ye get home later, ye can play."

"Will you be here, Conna?" Mike asked

"Yes, *mo gealachí*. Rick and I will be here when you get home."

The boys still didn't quite understand that the men lived there now, even though they saw them all the time. They'd yet to come into their bedroom at night or see either Rick or Conor kissing their mom. He heard the doorbell ring and went to let in Lilly.

Lilly scooped up the boys and gave Calleigh a kiss on the cheek. "Good morning." She saw that neither man was fully dressed for work. "Aren't you two going in to the office?"

"Not just yet, Lilly. We need te have a family discussion first," Conor said.

"Is that what they call it these days?" She looked at her daughter and saw the dark circles under her eyes. "Calleigh, as your mother, I'm ordering you after your family discussion to go to bed, for *sleeping* purposes only."

Calleigh laughed. "I promise, mom. I don't think anything else is even possible at this point." She gave each boy one last kiss and saw them out the door. She turned to face Rick and Conor. "Okay. Let's get this done. Then you can go to work, and I can go to bed." She walked over and flopped down on the sofa.

Rick and Conor walked over and sat on the large ottoman in front of the sofa. Calleigh looked so tired. Her normally bright complexion was dull, her hair was tied up in a messy knot, and her limbs looked disjointed. Rick hated to cause her further stress, but this was important.

"Calleigh, why didn't you tell us that Miles has been hassling you?" Rick asked.

"He wasn't doing anything threatening. Annoying, yes, but nothing I couldn't handle. He'd done nothing aggressive like this morning. If he had, I promise I would have told you."

"Well, thank God for that, but I still wish you would have said something. I know you're used to doing things for yourself, but you're not alone anymore. We're here for you, angel. We were your best friends long before we became your lovers. I don't want you to think that part of our relationship has changed."

Conor moved over to the sofa and placed his hand on Calleigh's cheek. "*Murinín*, if he's been blaggardin' ye in any way, I want ye to tell me. I want te stop it before ye get hurt. The thought of that fecking gobshite's hands on ye is twisting me up inside. We love ye."

"I love you both, too. I'm sorry. I didn't intend to keep it from you. Miles is all bluster. It's become widely known in the last month that he has a severe inferiority complex. I didn't know what he was really like when I accepted that date."

Rick joined them on the sofa on Calleigh's other side. "Angel, what about the threats he made before we left? Do you have any concerns?"

"No. I know I'm in the right at work, and the Social Services stuff is just ridiculous. We all know that there is nothing detrimental to the boys occurring in this house. Worst-case scenario, he calls and someone comes out for an interview. We explain the situation and let them see with their own eyes."

He stood and held out his hand. When Calleigh placed hers on his palm, he lifted her up and gave her a soft, chaste kiss. He rested his forehead against hers for a moment. "I love you, angel. Let's not do this again. My nerves can't take it." He smiled down at her.

Conor stood and pulled Calleigh into the circle of his arms. He gave her a soft kiss. "Let's get ye upstairs and in bed. How does a nice warm bath sound?"

"Heavenly. I'll draw one after you leave."

"No, *murinín*. We're on the hop today." He took her hand and led her upstairs.

# Chapter Seven

♥

While Conor was drawing Calleigh a bath, Rick went into the bedroom and pulled the blankets back. He found some scented oil in the nightstand drawer and drew the curtains over the windows to dampen the light in the room. They had a bluetooth speaker tucked onto a bookshelf in the corner, and he started one of Conor's Irish folk music playlists that included artists like Moya Brennan and Enya. The soothing instrumentals and harmonies of Celtic music always relaxed Rick. He'd never really appreciated his Irish heritage until Conor came along. Now, he embraced it more than anyone else in his immediate family. He looked up as Conor stepped into the room.

"Very nice. Yer thinking massage?" He stepped over and turned the volume down a little on the stereo.

Rick arranged the pillows on the bed to suit their needs. "Yeah. Thought it would be nice after the bath you drew. She's so exhausted she might fall asleep, but that's okay."

"I'll go see if she's ready te get out of the bath."

While Conor went to get Calleigh, Rick changed from work clothes into some comfortable lounging pants. He sat on the bed and waited for them to return. Conor carried Calleigh into the room and set her next to him. A big fluffy bath sheet covered her from shoulder to toes.

She looked around the room. "What's all this?"

Rick lifted the edge of the towel away. "We're going to give you a massage, then let you get some sleep." He slid her down the bed, so she was lying flat and rolled her onto her stomach. "Close your eyes, and let us take care of you."

Rick put some oil on his hands and rubbed them together. He handed the bottle over to Conor, who'd also changed. He started on the upper part of her back, while Conor focused on her feet. It must have felt good, because she let out a low groan.

Neither of them were experts, but Rick hoped his and Conor's hands soothed Calleigh. They smoothed the oil into her skin, and the scent of vanilla filled the air. Rick dug his fingers into tense muscles, and it seemed like tension melted from Calleigh's body, so he guessed they were doing something right. He worked his way down her back while Conor stayed on her feet, his thumbs digging into her arches.

"That feels so good."

Rick brushed his lips against the back of her neck. Calleigh squirmed a little, and that made him smile. She always went nuts when they kissed her neck. Conor's hands had moved up her calves and now massaged the top of her legs. His thumbs slid between her thighs. She spread her legs to give him more room. Time after time, his fingers grazed over her folds but did not advance. He placed kisses all over her bottom and dipped his tongue into her crease.

"Oh, please."

"Please what, *muirnín*?"

Calleigh squirmed, trying to get Conor's fingers to enter her. "Please touch me."

"We are touching you, angel," Rick whispered into her ear. One of his hands slid down her back and joined Conor's between her legs. He parted the folds, allowing only the very tip of his finger between them.

"I need more. I need all of you."

She wanted her men inside her, did she? Rick had no problem with that plan, although he hadn't intended for their pampering to turn sexual. He looked at Conor to get his reaction to Calleigh's plea. Conor aqua eyes trained on Calleigh's pussy, where their fingers played with the damp folds together. They each pushed forward and rubbed against her inner walls. Conor's finger slid alongside his inside their woman. They'd never double fucked one of their partners in the same hole before, but Rick's breath caught when he imagined how that might feel. Calleigh's hot wet channel embracing and rippling around their cocks as they slid against each other, fucking her simultaneously.

"Rick?"

He looked up at Conor and the silent question on his face. "I'm good. Just got a little caught up in a fantasy."

"Oh, yes. Do it, whatever you want, do it to me."

Rick chuckled. "Maybe someday, angel. But for right now, we'll make sure you're taken care of."

Calleigh pushed back against their fingers, seeking a deeper touch. Rick placed his hand on her back, stilling her movements.

"Noooo," she whined.

"It's okay, angel. We've got you." He turned her onto her side.

Conor laid down in front of her, his eyes bright, and his cheeks slashed with color. He lifted one of her legs over his hip and pushed his cock in deep. Calleigh's moans as Conor's slow rhythmic thrusts filled her body were music to his ears. She'd grasped his shoulders and tilted her hips forward. Rick watched as they shared a kiss. Conor's tongue slid inside her mouth. When their lips parted, Calleigh teased Conor and Rick saw the moment the man broke. His deep groan filled the room and the bed practically vibrated as he drove his hips in with a hard thrust.

He couldn't hold back any longer. Rick grabbed the bottle of lube from the bedside drawer and slicked up his fingers. Calleigh's warm silky skin brushed against his chest with every thrust of Conor's cock. Rick brushed his fingers against her back hole. The wrinkled skin relaxed to his probing fingers. He placed soft kisses on her neck. Rick slid a finger inside to the first knuckle. Calleigh tightened her muscles around his finger and Rick moaned. He needed to get his cock inside her. Needed to feel her heat surround him. He added a second finger to stretch her in preparation. Rick felt the length of Conor's cock thrust deep into Calleigh. God, he loved it when they had a woman between them like this. The push and pull of their bodies, scent of sex in the air, the cries of pleasure from all sides. He also knew just how to drive Conor crazy. Rick turned his fingers and pressed against the membrane separating them from Conor's cock, still thrusting in and out of Calleigh, causing both her and Conor to cry out. Conor drove deep inside her and stilled.

Rick pulled his fingers out and slicked up his cock. He pushed against her asshole. He gave Calleigh a second to adjust to the brief sting that always came with sharing your body with another person in this way, then slid deep inside her. All three of them groaned in the darkened room, their low moans a symphony in the heated silence. Calleigh turned her head to look over her shoulder and Rick captured her mouth in a kiss. He thrust his tongue inside, capturing her sighs as he pushed his cock deep into her tight body.

"So perfect," he whispered hoarsely. "So beautiful the way you open yourself for our love, angel."

Calleigh moaned and leaned into Conor's chest. Rick took a few slow plunges, and she panted.

"God, Calleigh," Rick gasped, His hands tightened on her hips as he slowly filled her over and over. "So tight. So hot."

His thickness slid all the way inside her and added to the fullness of Conor in front. Rick reached around her and stroked her open pussy gently, teasing her inflamed clit until she moaned and her inner muscles trembled.

"Ghawd all feckin' mighty!" Conor cried.

Conor's cock retreated almost all the way out, so that only the head remained inside her, then shoved inwards again, hard. He and Conor enclosed Calleigh in their arms. The three of them shared such a primal connection when they came together like this. He looked at Conor over Calleigh's shoulder. The man's face was flushed, beads of sweat dotted his forehead, and with every thrust of his body into Calleigh's, the cords on his neck stood out.

"You ready?" He asked. Conor's eyes flashed open and Rick found himself trapped by their stare for a few heartbeats.

"Let's bring her home."

Rick withdrew until only the head of his cock was inside Calleigh. Conor did the same, and they paused at her entrances. They'd done this together for so many years, the two of them communicated without words as they prepared to send Calleigh into the stratosphere of ecstasy. He could read Conor's body so well that Rick matched his tempo, driving into Calleigh in a measured thrusts.

As a unit, they claimed the deepest parts of Calleigh's body. Breathy little pants escaped as she lay between them. Conor's tender lilt merged with his dark whispers against Calleigh's skin. All his brain could process was the feel of the pull and push of their cocks into the woman they loved. He took Calleigh's cheeks in both hands and pulled them apart. Rick watched as she swallowed him whole as he shuttled his cock into her over and over again, catapulting him straight into heaven. He thrust once. Twice. Long, deep strokes that reached inside him and strangled his cock. His balls slapped against Conor's, sending shocks of rapture shooting through him.

"Oh God ... Oh please..." Calleigh moaned.

Rick's gripped her hips as he ground into her ass, and Conor's fingers played with her nipples as he thrust hard and deep. The slow wave built inside him. The pleasure insane. More than Rick ever thought possible to experience before. He couldn't contain it. Desperate to get Calleigh to the pinnacle, he used every trick in the book to stimulate her body. Pushing her higher and higher. She made soft, helpless sounds. They sped up their rhythm.

"*Muirnín*," Conor murmured in her ear, thrusting inside her. "*Tá ar chroís istigh ionat.*"

"God, Calleigh," Rick whispered, slamming into her back passage. "Conor is right. Our hearts are within you."

Calleigh nearly sobbed. She reached up to cup Conor's cheek, then back to stroke Rick's. "Love you both so much."

Rick breathed against the back of her neck as they moved in rapid accord, driving deep inside her. The wave reached a crest, his entire body spasmed. Euphoria poured out of him like a raging inferno. It ravaged him, burning him to a crisp, turning him inside out. Somewhere in the recess of his mind, he heard Calleigh cry out and her spasms joined theirs as both he and Conor released inside her.

Calleigh ran the vacuum across the area rug in the living room. She had to finish before Kevin's mother, Susan, arrived. A set of arms wrapped around her, and she identified the scent belonging to Rick.

"You doing okay, angel?"

She leaned back into his embrace. The last few days leading up to the anniversary of Kevin's death had been difficult. She'd been seeking comfort from Rick and Conor more, clutching them at night. She knew that an examination of her motives would show her subconscious fear of their deaths, making her cling to them more.

"I'm okay. Thank you for agreeing to visit Kevin with us. I plan on telling Susan tonight at dinner."

"You asked. Of course, we'd go." He placed a kiss on her temple and turned her around to give her another one on her lips.

"I hope you and Conor have fun at the game tonight."

"I'll have a good soccer game, a pint of Guinness and my best friend. The only thing missing is my girl. "

Conor walked in at that moment and wrapped his arms around Calleigh's back. "Our girl." He kissed the back of her neck. "It's cold enough to freeze the balls off a brass monkey, but we promise not te come home all gee-eyed." He looked at Rick. "We'd better be goin'."

They bundled up in coats and scarves. Calleigh gave them one last kiss and sent her big boys out to play.

A few hours later, Calleigh, Susan, Mikey, and Brandon were sitting in the restaurant. Conversation had comprised Susan's trip and the boys filling her in on their most recent adventures.

Susan looked over at her daughter-in-law. "Calleigh, I can't believe how much they've grown. And they're talking so much."

Calleigh was sitting between her sons and ruffled their blond heads. "I know. It seems like their vocabulary has tripled in the last six months. Mostly, you can have simple conversations with them about anything happening around us. Although sometimes they have to remind me to say things in a kid way. Their preschool is fantastic. They really nurture social skills."

Susan set her glass of wine down on the table and twirled the stem. "So tell me. How are you doing?"

Calleigh finished cutting Mikey's chicken tenders so they could cool. "I'm doing really well, actually. These few days are always going to be tough, but mostly, we're just living our lives the best way we can."

They continued to discuss the boys and other national and world matters until the server removed their plates. Calleigh enjoyed herself but knew she had to broach the subject of Rick and Conor accompanying them to the cemetery tomorrow. Maybe if she ducked out to the ladies' room for a moment, she could gather her courage. She took Mikey and Brandon's coloring books and crayons out of her ever-present bag and placed them in front of each boy.

"Susan, would you mind watching the boys for a moment? I need to step out to the ladies' room."

"Of course. I was wondering, Calleigh, are you dating again?"

She stopped as she was about to leave the table and took a deep breath. "Actually yes. I started dating a couple of months ago and have something I wish to speak to you about, but first, I really *do* need to use the ladies' room. Will you excuse me?"

"Of course. Take your time."

She felt Susan's eyes on her as she practically ran from the table. Turning, she saw the boys were both watching her.

He used the facilities and headed back toward the table. Calleigh was behind a pillar out of sight of the table when she caught the sound of boys' conversation with Susan. She peered around the pillar to not spy on them. She'd never spy on her kids.

"M*amó, I glad you here.*"

"Mikey, what did you call me?"

"*Mamó,*" Brandon responded

"But sweeties, I'm grandma." She looked at both boys as they nodded. "Have you met your mommy's new friend?" More nods. "Is he nice to you?"

Brandon looked back down at the picture he was coloring. "Ah-huh. Conna read stories good."

Mike picked up a new crayon. "Wick plays cars with us."

"Brandon did you say Rick, and Michael what name did you say?"

"Conner. Sorry I try to say my 'R' wight. Con-ner helps me pwactice what Ms. Emma teach me at school."

Calleigh smiled. They'd started both boys in speech therapy a couple of months ago. The speech pathologist assured her most of their errors were age appropriate, but there were a few others that needed to be addressed. Rick, Conor, and she did their best to reinforce the lessons the boys had while at their pre-school.

"What would you boys like for breakfast before we go visit your father tomorrow?"

"Wick make smiley takes," they said simultaneously.

It was probably time to intervene. She came around the pillar and saw Susan straightening the debris on the table.

"Boys, put your coloring books away." Susan ordered.

Susan stood and picked up their coats. Calleigh had thought to have this conversation in a public place, hoping that the venue would prevent Susan from making a scene, but maybe this was better. It really was a private matter.

"Did the boys want to go?" She asked, trying to making it seem like she absolutely hadn't been spying on the table.

"I think it's time we got them home. We can have that discussion there."

"Well, okay." Calleigh kneeled in front of her sons. "Do either of you need to use the potty?" Twin heads shook. "Are you sure?" They nodded. "Okay, we'll go when we get home."

"They're potty training already?"

Calleigh stood and faced Susan. "We started just after they turned three. It's going pretty well, but sometimes we still have accidents. Especially when we're out having fun and distracted from listening to our bodies. They're getting better at telling me. I always ask before we leave anywhere, so they get the idea."

When they arrived at the house, Calleigh got both boys out of the car seats and hurried them inside. The night air was frigid. She hoped Rick and Conor were okay. She was sure if the temperature dropped much more, they would head to a pub close to campus.

"Okay, boys. Coats in the closet and go upstairs for PJ time. Meet me in the bathroom to go potty and brush your teeth." She looked over at her mother-in-law. "Susan, make yourself comfortable. I'll be down in a few minutes."

She was very proud of her boys when they went to the bathroom. Both of them were dry, and they each got a gold star on the potty chart.

They were saving their stars for a Hot Wheels race track. Mike and Brandon tugged on their Spiderman pajamas, and they all went back downstairs. She settled them in their playroom off the kitchen, and she started some coffee. Once finished, she carried the two cups into the living room. The first sip made Calleigh wince, and she set the cup down to cool for a moment.

"So Susan, is there anything in particular you'd like to do tomorrow after we visit Kevin?"

"Actually, I wanted to talk to you about something else first. I was talking with Michael and Brandon at the restaurant, and they said two different names for your new friend. What is his name?"

"Susan, I'm not sure how I feel about you asking Mikey and Brandon about my boyfriends?"

"All I asked was if they had met him and was he nice to them. What do you mean 'boyfriends'? Are you dating more than one? Wouldn't that be confusing to the boys to introduce a new man all the time?"

"Susan, I appreciate your concern, but I think I understand the boys and their limitations better than you. I know you love them, but they are extremely bright and generally ahead of the curve for age-appropriate behavior. However, this is as good a time as any to speak to you about tomorrow. I've invited both Conor and Rick to go with us to the cemetery. Both men are invaluable friends and have been there for both the boys and me over the past three years."

"I'm glad you had friends to help you through this. So this Conor and Rick, they're the ones Michael and Brandon were speaking of?"

"Yes. They're my best friends, and the boys look to them as father figures." She took a deep breath because this was going to be the hardest part. "They are also the men I'm dating."

For several heartbeats, the room was silent. Susan's face was a stone mask. Calleigh tried to put herself in that position. Here she visited on the anniversary of her son's death and her former daughter-in-law had told her she not only had moved on and was dating again, but was part of a ménage á trois.

"I don't understand, Calleigh."

"Conor, Rick, and I are a throuple. The three of us have a special relationship where we are all equal partners. I am not dating only Rick or only Conor. I am dating them both, and they are both dating me. In fact, they live here. Our intention is to blend the three of us, Michael, Brandon, and any future children into a complete family."

More silence filled the space. Calleigh heard the sounds of the boys playing in the other room. Plastic trucks were crashing against each other, and they were making screeching and crashing noises.

"I know this must seem like a shock, but please understand, we are happy. The boys have two surrogate fathers who love them as their own. I'm happy in this relationship. It's not better than what Kevin and I shared. It's just different. Rick and Conor will be a part of this family from now on, and I hope you can accept their roles in the boys' lives. They will not wipe Kevin's memory from this house. They are enriching our lives in the space he left behind."

Calleigh watched as Susan's face turned red, her fists clenched and her eyes took on a shockingly bright fever.

"You filthy whore! You Satan's mistress. You disgust me! I will not allow your deviant behavior to taint my son's children."

Her ears rang from Susan's high-pitched voice, screaming in the small room. "Stop right there, Susan! I understand this being a shock to you, but do not for a single second think you have any say in how I raise my children. My behavior is not deviant or immoral. It's a lifestyle choice—one you may not understand or agree with. Regardless, I decide how to raise *my* children, and I choose to raise them in a loving and nurturing home with three adults."

By now, she was raising her voice and attempted to restrain from getting any louder. She did not want to alarm the boys. "Another thing. Kevin would accept this relationship and be grateful that our children have the love and support they need and deserve. I know this because a marriage of three was not a foreign concept to him ... or us."

Calleigh's head snapped around at the force of the slap from Susan's open palm. Her ears rang, and little lights danced in front of her eyes for a moment.

"Don't you ever speak such filth about my son! He was a God-fearing man. A national hero. He died for this country in a squalid desert, and you repay him by whoring yourself and exposing his children to disgusting perverts!"

The front door slammed open. Conor and Rick came running in and stopped in the entryway to the living room. Their eyes locked, and Calleigh was thankful for the low light. They wouldn't be able to see her face, but she was sure a bright red handprint glowed on her cheek.

"I will not stand for this. I am going to collect my grandchildren and take them away from you people. You've made a huge mistake, Calleigh. I'll have you declared an unfit mother by the courts and gain custody so fast it'll make your head spin." She turned around and spied two men standing in the doorway. "And you perverts ... keep your filthy hands off my grandchildren. God only knows what horrors you've already made them witness or even take part in."

Susan started walking toward the back playroom. Calleigh moved to stop her, but Rick beat her to it. He reached out and grasped Susan by the upper arm and spun her around.

"You will leave this house immediately. I will not stand for you treating Calleigh in such a manner. You have no idea what our relationship is like. Not one of us would ever do anything to hurt those precious little boys. They are the light of our world. It's bigoted spiteful bitches like you who propagate such lies. There are thousands of loving and committed alternate lifestyle relationships raising families in this country. In fact, most of those children develop into more stable adults than those raised in what you consider a normal home."

Susan jerked her arm out of the man's grip. "I'm calling the police and you'll be hearing from my lawyer!"

Calleigh heard Conor mutter something in Gaelic. His scowl and voice betrayed his disdain for her mother-in-law. She watched the woman she had, if not loved, always respected as Kevin's mother. She'd always known Kevin's parents screwed toward conservative beliefs, but did not know the woman was so narrow minded. Calleigh couldn't believe Susan thought they would hurt the boys or molest them. Just the thought made Calleigh sick. Then she realized she really was going to be sick. She sprinted past Conor and Rick for the powder room off the kitchen. Opening the door, she stumbled to her knees and barely got the toilet seat up before heaving the contents of her supper into the porcelain bowl. Her stomach continued to cramp even after nothing more came up as dry heaves racked her body.

Conor dampened a soft cloth and kneeled behind Calleigh. His hand rubbed in slow circles as he placed the cloth on the back of her neck. "*Muirnín*. Please donna do this te yerself. We willna let anything happen te our family. I swear te ye."

When Calleigh's body stopped jerking, he wiped her mouth with the damp cloth. He handed her a glass of water so she could wash out her mouth. Sitting back on his heels, he gathered her into his arms.

He felt the coolness of her skin and wrapped his arms around her tighter to transfer as much heat as possible. Trembles took over her body, and she clutched his shirt as he rubbed her back and whispered soothing words in her ear.

Finally, she pulled back, and he got a look at her face in the light of the sconces on the bathroom wall. A livid mark in the shape of a hand ran across her left cheek. Seeing evidence of violence on Calleigh made him see red. That vile woman had hurt his sweetheart. He reached up and gently touched the mark, and his heart twisted when he saw Calleigh wince. Leaning down, he placed a soft kiss on her cheek.

"I'm sorry she hurt ye, *mo ghrá*. Let's get ye some ice for that and check on the rest of our family. Rick went to check on Mikey and Bran. I'm sure they want a hug from ye."

They stood and walked into the living room. Rick sat in the club chair and had both boys in his lap, encased in his arms. Their heads rested on his chest, and Conor saw tear tracks on their cheeks.

"Come give yer ma a hug, little ones."

They looked up simultaneously and scampered off Rick's lap to run into their mother's arms. Calleigh gathered both boys to her and held them tight. She smoothed their hair and kissed their foreheads. His little lights were distraught, and it was all that *cailleach's* fault. The witch poisoned this house of love with her evil brew.

He didn't think either boy wanted to be away from their ma right now, but he could tell the little ones were about to fall asleep in her arms. "I don't know about ye, but I'm knackered. Why don't we have a camp out here in the livin' room the-night. The whole family."

"That's a great idea, Conor." Calleigh smiled up at him. "We can get the air mattresses and have a slumber party."

"She's right. Just what our family needs tonight. Mikey and Bran, why don't you come with me to get the blankets and pillows?" Rick gave Conor's shoulder a squeeze as they left the room.

Not long after that, they were all lying on the pillows of air. He and Rick were on the outside edges. Next came the boys, and Calleigh was in the middle of everyone. The boys were sound asleep, and Conor opened his eyes one last time to see Calleigh looking at him.

*Thank you*, she mouthed.

*I love ye, muirnín,* he mouthed back.

# Chapter Eight

♥

**M**ikey opened his eyes as the sun came through the window. He looked around the room and saw Brandon next to him on the mattress. They often ended up sleeping together when scared. Last night had been scary. Grandma and mommy were yelling, and Rick and Conor didn't look happy, but he didn't understand what had happened. At first, he'd thought Grandma had been mad at him. She kept yelling his and Brandon's names. When the yelling had stopped, he went to find mommy, but she was gone. He was scared that she had left them. Rick had gathered up him and Brandon and sat in the chair. He told them the grown-ups were having a disagreement, but they weren't mad at them. Mikey liked it when Rick held him in his lap. He was so big and always warm to cuddle with.

He looked next to him and saw Brandon's eyes open and watching him. He knew Brandon had been scared last night, too. They didn't need to talk to understand what the other was thinking or feeling. Somehow, they always knew. He sat up and crawled to the edge of the mattress. He didn't want to wake up mommy, Rick or Conor. Brandon was right behind him. They walked into the playroom. He picked up their trucks and held them out to his brother.

"You want to play?"

Brandon shook his head no. Mikey looked around and pointed to the box of blocks. Again, Brandon wasn't interested. Mikey saw him grab the front of his pants and pull. He knew what that meant. Taking his brother's hand, he led him to the bathroom. He stared at the potty. They didn't have their step stools or seats down here. Brandon was dancing around. Mike was trying to figure out how to make this work when Brandon pushed him. He watched as his brother pushed his pants off, climbed up to his knees on the seat, put his hands on the back of the potty and started peeing. He didn't know you could do that. When Brandon was done, he did the same and felt much better afterwards.

"Where you 'earn that?"

"Conna show me. I see him do it. He was on his feet."

"I hungy. Let's get mommy."

They walked into the living room, and he giggled at all the grown-ups. They were in a pile on the floor. Conor and Rick had mommy squished between them. He pointed and Brandon giggled, too. Rick moved and gave mommy a hug. He turned his head and kissed her. Mike had never seen Rick kiss mommy before. He looked over at Brandon and saw that he was watching, too. When he looked back, he saw Conor talking softly to mommy then he kissed her, too.

"Why you kiss mommy?"

Rick froze. He'd forgotten they weren't in their bedroom. He'd woken up to feel Calleigh's soft body next to him and reacted as he did every morning. Hearing one of the boys' voices catapulted him into wakefulness. He sat up on the mattress to see them standing next to each other at the archway between the kitchen and living room. Calleigh and Conor were sitting up as well, and they all looked at each other with questions on how to handle this one on their faces. He decided to explain everything to the boys.

"Come here, boys." He patted the mattress next to him.

They walked over and crawled across the mattress. Michael sat next to him and Brandon sat on the other side of Calleigh between her and Conor.

"I kissed your mommy because I love her and so does Conor." He saw the confusion on the boys' faces. "Do you know what it means for a man and woman to be married?" Both boys nodded their heads. "Well Conor and I want to marry your mom. You know we've been around a lot more lately, but what Conor and I both really want is to be a family. The two of you, your mom, me and Conor."

The boys didn't say anything, but he could see they were processing what he'd said. Especially Mikey. He was the thinker of the two, always plotting out what he wanted to do before acting. Brandon tended to act first and deal with effects afterward. But they surprised him this time.

"Will you be our daddy?" Brandon asked.

Rick's heart flipped around in his chest at such a simple question. He and Conor already loved the boys as their own, but to hear them call him 'daddy' stirred him deep inside.

"Would you like that? Do you want to call us daddy?" His voice sounded hoarse to his ears.

The two boys looked at each other for a minute, doing that silent twin communication thing they did so often. He held his breath but refused to rush them. Then they both turned to look at him and nodded their heads in unison. Tears gathered in his eyes and he held out his arms. "Come here, sons. Can you give your new daddy a hug?"

He gathered their small bodies in his arms and pulled them onto his lap. Little hearts were beating in their chests and small fingers dug into his shirt. He looked up to see Calleigh smiling with bright, happy eyes. Tears ran down her cheeks. He looked at Conor and saw the man's desire to hold his sons as well.

"Why don't you go over and give your other dad a hug, too. I'm sure he would love that."

They jumped and bounced across the mattress to launch themselves into Conor's arms. After a hard hug, Conor leaned back. Mikey and Brandon were each straddling one of his legs, and he was supporting them behind their backs.

Conor looked at both boys. "Ye *gasurs* are the lights of me life. I love ye so much. Brandon ye are like sunlight. Always bright and happy, filling our days with your energy. That's why I call you *mo grian*, which means my sun and Michael you are like moonlight. Reflective and beautiful, ever changing and guiding our lives. That's why I call you *mo gealachí*, which means my moon. I would love for ye te call me Da. That 'tis how we say dad in Ireland. Can ye do that for me?"

Both boys nodded and started jumping up and down on the mattress and cheering. Calleigh's face turned gray, and she put a hand up to her mouth. She leapt over Rick and raced towards the bathroom. He followed and found her bent over the toilet. After cleaning her up, he lifted her in his arms and carried her into the kitchen, where Conor was making the boys' breakfast. He caught their gazes with the question plain in his eyes.

Rick set her down on a chair at the table and pulled up another beside her. "That's the second time in two days, Calleigh." He put a hand to her forehead but felt nothing except cool, clammy skin.

"I'm fine, Rick. Last night was just from anxiety and stress. I'm sure this morning was just lingering effects."

"Is there any chance it could be something else? We never asked you about protection. From Conor's and my perspective, it wasn't important, but I realize that was selfish of us. So I apologize."

He leaned over and kissed her softly, then heard giggles from the other side of the table and realized it would take the boys a little while before they got used to seeing displays of affection between them.

She placed her hand on his cheek. "I would love to have another child. I can't think of anything better than to know we created a life out of the love I share with you and Conor, but I know that's not the case. To regulate my menstrual cycles, I use birth control shots. Have since Mike and Brandon were born. I know a lot of women have switched over to IUDs, but since I wasn't sexually active, I didn't see the reason. Now that the three of us are together, I'll probably ask my OBGYN which one would be the best option. Anyway, I administered my last shot a week before we got together, so I know I'm protected for another month."

"Okay, angel, I guess a small part of me hoped that could be it. Promise me if you feel any worse, you'll see a doctor? I couldn't bear it if this was something more, and we did nothing to help you. This family needs you."

"I promise. Now, let's have a nice family breakfast because I'm sure this is only the calm before the storm."

A beam of moonlight shone through the bow windows in their bedroom. Calleigh watched the sheer curtain flutter as the heat kicked on. She couldn't sleep. In fact, she felt smothered lying between Conor and Rick. She moved to climb over Conor. As Calleigh poised above him, Conor snaked his arms around her and pulled her down so their bodies were flush. She could tell he was still asleep by the deep, even breaths escaping his mouth. She was stuck straddling his hips as he thrust them against her. He mumbled something incoherent, and she dropped a small kiss to his lips. A moment later, his arms fell back to his sides, and she climbed off the side of the bed.

Picking up her robe, she slipped her arms through the soft material and tiptoed out the bedroom door. She checked on the boys, then crept downstairs. Sitting in the club chair by the bow windows in the living room, she stared out into the night. The cars shimmered with a layer of frost in the streetlamps.

She was exhausted, but couldn't seem to get her mind to shut down. For the past week, her emotions had bounced from one extreme to another. She had floated the entire day the first morning Mike and Brandon had spontaneously called Rick and Conor dad. The next day, she got a call from her supervisor at the hospital saying Miles had filed a complaint of sexual harassment against her. Rick and Conor had blown a gasket over that one. The boys were making excellent progress in the potty training. The other day she had gone to get them out of bed and found them already in the bathroom, pulling down their pajama pants.

Rick and Conor had questioned her at dinner tonight, because she had had little appetite. It didn't help that she was still intermittently throwing up. Sometimes, she just ended up dry heaving because of the lack of food in her system. She hadn't told Rick and Conor because she knew they would worry. She knew the culprit was stress. When she looked in the mirror before getting to bed, she saw dark circles under her puffy eyes and her hair looked limp. No wonder they hadn't wanted to make love to her all week. Daily harassing calls from Susan put a pall over the household. The temptation to block her number was strong, but Calleigh just couldn't bring herself to do it. She had stopped answering.

The last voicemail Susan had left said that she'd gotten a lawyer and going to sue for custody. She'd even mentioned contacting a representative from the Department of Children and Families to file a report of abuse. Calleigh prayed every day that they couldn't take her precious babies away. She knew there was no evidence of physical or emotional neglect, but one never knew how government services could twist things to suit their needs. Could Susan take her children?

Didn't the courts always side with mother, except in extreme cases? Not for one second did Calleigh question her choice of staying with Rick and Conor. She needed them like air and was determined to make this work. She heard a creak and looked up to see Conor descending the stairs.

"*Muirnín*? Why are ye down here instead of in bed with us?"

"Couldn't sleep. Didn't want to wake either of you."

He picked up a throw blanket on the back of the sofa and walked over to the chair. Lifting Calleigh up, he sat, then settled her on his lap and tucked the blanket around them. "Ye wanna talk?"

She shook her head. "Too much jumbled in there to sort out right now. Will you just hold me for a little while?"

"I'll always hold ye, *mo ghrá*. Put yer head down and try te get some sleep."

As Calleigh's eyes drifted shut, he softly hummed one of his favorite Irish lullabies. He frequently did so for the boys when they had trouble going down, and it seemed to work on their mom as well. Calleigh had thought he was asleep when he'd tried to keep her in bed earlier, but he knew the moment she crawled over him that she was trying to escape.

She hadn't slept through a night this week and it showed. He knew she was still getting sick, too. She had tried to keep it from them, but Carla had called one evening to ask if Calleigh was feeling better since she'd gotten sick earlier at work. Once or twice, he could understand from stress, but this had moved beyond that.

He looked down and realized she was finally out. Her breathing was even, and her head was limp against his chest. He rose, carrying her back upstairs. When he reached the side of the bed, Rick was awake.

"She get sick again?" Rick whispered.

"No, just sitting down by the windy staring out into the night," he whispered back.

Rick helped him get her robe off, and he gently laid her down on the bed. He climbed in next to her and rolled onto his back. Pulling up the covers, he tucked them around her. He put his arms behind his head and he stared up at the decorative ceiling medallion. "We need te do something. She canny keep goin' like this. The boys are startin' te notice, too."

"I know. Let me think on it some. Try and get some sleep. It'll be another long day tomorrow."

# Chapter Nine

♥

R ick picked up the phone in his office and dialed the number he'd found online. He hoped a call to one of their friends from Boston College would provide some answers. As he waited for the line to connect, he fiddled with the screen shot suggestions for that new Olympic game they were working on. The art department was working on background effects before adding in the code for play. This one was a half-pipe competition, and he noticed that one spectator held up an Irish flag, but the colors were in the wrong order. He smiled because he knew Conor would have a fit if he saw that. He was about to give up when the line connected.

"United States Attorney's office. How can I help you?"

"This is Richard Connor. May I please speak with Ethan Harrison?" He leaned back in his chair as the assistant connected him. A few moments later, the cheerful voice of his friend transmitted through the line.

"Rick? How the hell are you?"

"I'm good. How've you been? I know we haven't talked in a couple of months, sorry. What's new?"

"Same old, same old. How's my favorite gingernut?"

"He'd kick your scrawny ass if he heard you call him that," Rick said, smiling.

"I know, I know, ''Tis not red, ye arse'."

He laughed at Ethan's spot-on imitation. "As much as I wish this were a purely social call, we have a situation I wanted to get your take on."

"That never sounds good. Shoot. Then we can get back to the fun stuff."

"Well, it's like this. Conor and I have finally found our third."

"Please tell me you two finally grew a pair and told Calleigh how you feel?"

"How did you—"

"Seriously? The two of you have been more transparent than windows for the past year. Any time you've talked about her or those little boys, the fact that you're madly in love has been obvious."

Rick couldn't decide if he wanted to smile, roll his eyes, or sigh. So he kind of did all three. "Okay, yes. Calleigh, Conor, and I are together. Anyway, her mother-in-law flipped when she found out about our relationship and is threatening to sue for custody and get DFC involved. It's turned Calleigh into a wreck. What I was wondering is, can the mother-in-law succeed based solely on our relationship?"

"I would love to razz you some more, but I'll save it for another day. Listen, no judge would take away children from a parent based solely on a moral objection from the third party. As long as you can prove the children are being provided for and living in a healthy home, you shouldn't have any problems."

"Thank God. I really didn't think it was possible, but you never know. So how's your love life? Seeing anyone?"

"Unfortunately, my quest for love has hit a dead end. The last couple of dates I went on were disastrous. I swear you'd think I could find one decent man in the city of Boston. Is tall, hot, built, smart and desperately in love with me really too much to ask for?"

Rick laughed. "No, my friend. I'm sure you'll find him. I'll keep my eye out for you. You know, it's been way too long since we really hung out. Why don't I call you when this all calms down, and you can meet the family?"

"Sounds good, buddy. My assistant just poked her head in and told me my next client is waiting, so I got to run. Give my best to Conor. Tell that crazy mick he still owes me a margarita since I drank that nasty brew he calls beer on St. Paddy's."

"Will do. See ya, Ethan."

After he hung up, he felt much better. In fact, he felt as if an immense weight had lifted from his shoulders. He picked up the phone to call Conor and share the news, but then looked at the clock. Five o'clock approached. He could tell him on the way home.

He caught the elevator down to the lobby, and Conor was waiting in their usual spot. "You ready to head home?"

"Actually, I need te run a few errands. Phil called and said he finished the setting today. So I thought I'd stop by on the way 'ome and pick it up. I'll snag dinner so we don't have te worry about cookin'."

"Excellent. Then I'll meet Calleigh at the hospital when she gets off shift. I have some news to share with the family tonight also, so don't be too late. Lilly is picking up the boys from after school care and should be home by seven o'clock."

The Boston traffic gods were in his favor and Rick made it to the hospital in decent time. He'd just climbed out of the car and walked around the back end when Calleigh walked out the doors of the massive complex. When she saw him, a huge smile lit up her face, and she ran into his arms. Gathering her close, he buried his head in her neck and inhaled. Her scent lingered beneath the hospital odors clinging to her scrubs. Pulling back, he leaned in for a kiss.

He'd intended for it to be brief, but once his lips touched hers, he couldn't hold back. They were soft and felt so perfect against him. His tongue licked across the seam, and she opened to let him inside. He loved the sweet taste of his angel. His tongue slipped between her lips again and again. His arms slid around her waist, pulling her in tight. Calleigh latched her arms around his neck, holding him close.

He pressed his erection against her soft belly. Days had passed since he'd been inside her, and the stress induced suppression of his desires disintegrated. He needed her. Now. Spirals of heat streaked through his bloodstream. Calleigh's tongue dipped into his mouth and flicked over his teeth. The tangling of their flesh stoked the molten desire racing through him. He loosened his grip on her, and she moaned.

Separating their lips, he panted, "I need you, angel. It's been too long. Where can we go?"

She looked around for a moment, then grabbed his hand. Pulling him inside the hospital, they walked through an 'employees only' door and slipped inside a private bathroom. He flipped the lock on the door and pushed Calleigh against the painted wall across from the sink.

"I'm sorry, angel, but this won't be wine and romance."

She pushed down her scrubs as he ripped open his belt and dress pants. They fell to his ankles. Their mouths latched together once again, and he reached around to grab her ass. Lifting her up, her legs wrapped around his waist, he balanced her against the wall and reached down to see if she was wet enough to accept him. The evidence of her desire coated his fingers, and he groaned into her mouth. Slipping two digits inside her snug heat made her gasp.

"Please, Rick. I need."

"I know what you need, angel. Don't worry, I'll take care of you."

He held his cock and fit it to her entrance. In a single thrust, he slid home and captured Calleigh's cry with his lips. The hot, tight, wet channel gripping him was too much, and he started fucking her. Calleigh's nails dug into his shoulders. His eyes bored into hers. Her hot breath panted against his lips. He started hammering into her, driving himself deeper into the heaven of her body. Whimpers escaped, even though she tried to hold them back. His hips jack-knifed, and the pull of her muscles against his cock sent unspeakable pleasure racing down his spine. Suddenly, her body tensed and the ripples of her orgasm locked him deep inside. He cried out as his climax was ripped from the marrow of his bones. Pulsing, shaking, shuddering, the explosion went on forever.

When he regained his faculties, he realized he still had her pinned to the wall. He heard her hiss as he separated their flesh. Concern immediately replaced his lingering pleasure.

"Angel, are you all right? Was I too rough?"

"No, love. That was exactly what I needed."

He leaned in and kissed her again. He never got enough of her sweet lips. After several lingering soft kisses, he pulled back. Stooping, he helped her get back into her scrubs and tided himself.

"Let's go home."

They just beat Conor back to the house. Lilly had dropped off the boys, the left quickly citing the need to get to her book club meeting. Conor's hello kiss lasted longer than normal. When he and Calleigh finally separated, he locked his gaze on Rick's and he knew the other man had caught the scent of their lovemaking on Calleigh's body.

"Did ye two just get home?"

"Yes, we had a bit of a delay at the hospital."

Conor chuckled. "I'll bet." He looked back down at his love. "*Muirnín*, you look much better tonight. Your eyes have their glow back and your cheeks have color in them again." He leaned over to whisper in her ear. "I can smell Rick on ye, *mo ghrá*. Knowing the two of ye made love is gonna leave me gummin'. I canny wait to get ye in bed the-night. I'm goin' te lick every inch of this beautiful body, then slide deep inside ye until ye shudder all around me."

Rick smiled when he saw Calleigh blush at Conor's whispered promise. He inhaled deeply as he opened the bags Conor had brought home. The scents of chicken modiga from their favorite restaurant wafted up, and his mouth watered. He set the table and got the boys corralled into their booster chairs. He set their sippy cups filled with milk in front of them while Calleigh cut up their chicken fingers to cool.

"I even brought home some afters for us te enjoy lay-ra."

Calleigh leaned over and gave Conor a kiss on the cheek. "I love dessert, thank you. What did you bring home?"

"It's a surprise, *mo ghrá*. After Mikey an' Bran are asleep, the three of us can relax an' enjoy the treat."

Rick figured this was the perfect time to tell Conor and Calleigh about his conversation with Ethan earlier. He took a sip of his wine and looked up to get their attention.

"I placed a call today to an old friend of Conor's and mine from college. He specializes in securities law, but is familiar enough with family law that I trust what he says."

Conor rolled his eyes. "Why dinna I think of callin' grapenuts?"

"Who?" Calleigh asked.

"Never mind him, angel. Our buddy's name is Ethan Harrison. He's an assistant attorney for the U.S. Attorney's office here in Boston. Anyway, he said we really should have nothing to worry about from Susan. He assured me that a judge would not remove a child from a home strictly based on a moral disagreement between parties. There would have to be evidence of neglect."

He looked at Calleigh and saw the relief on her face at his announcement. He had been worried she would be upset he'd gone behind her back, but it appeared she appreciated his initiative.

She stood and went over to hug Rick, holding him tight for a moment. "Thank you. I can't tell you how much better I feel. It's nice to have someone with actual legal experience confirm my suspicions."

"Good on ye. I haven't talked to Ethan in donkey's years! How is the rossie?"

"He says you still owe him a frozen margarita for making him drink that pint of Arthur's last Paddy's."

Conor laughed. "The man never could stand the black stuff."

They finished their dinner, and he and Conor took Mikey and Brandon upstairs for baths and story time. After settling everyone for the night, Rick stopped Conor in the upstairs hallway. "Did you get it?"

Conor held out the small box and lifted the lid. The light from the hallway reflected off the diamond engagement ring they had picked out for Calleigh. Conor had explained to the jeweler what design he wanted for the setting, and he had chosen the stone. The platinum band had a series of trinity knots, a classic Celtic design, along the shoulders and at the center, a princess cut diamond. It had a matching wedding band with trinity knots inset into the band.

"It's perfect, Con."

"Are ye sure? It's not too Irish for ye? I dinna want ye te feel like—"

"Conor, stop. You may have thicker Irish blood running through your veins, but I come from Shannon, too. Those trinity knots are three interlaced triangles that represent unending love. I can't think of a better symbol for our lives with Calleigh than what you have in your hand."

He pulled Conor into a tight, reassuring hug. Their friendship, built on a shared love for Calleigh and their commitment to the same way of life, had woven their paths together. When he pulled back, he noticed a glimmer of moisture in Conor's eyes, and felt the same sting in his own. From the moment their bond had formed in college, their relationship had shifted in ways neither could have predicted. Rick didn't know what the future held, but there was one thing he knew for sure: he had always loved this man, and he always would.

Calleigh put the last dish away in the cabinet and turned on the coffeemaker. The rich aromatic scent of hazelnut filled the kitchen. Walking into the living room, she kneeled beside the hearth and lit the kindling in the fireplace. The crackle of the dried wood and the warmth of the flame were soothing. She turned her head as she heard footsteps on the stairs and saw Rick and Conor enter the room.

"Are they ready for me?"

"Yes, angel, go say goodnight, then come back down so we can enjoy that dessert Conor brought home."

She rose from her knees and gave each man a soft kiss before heading upstairs to give her babies a final tuck in. Opening the door to their bedroom, she found they were both already asleep. She leaned over and tucked the blankets tighter around Brandon—he tended to thrash around at night—and placed a kiss on his forehead. Slipping over to the other side of the room, she picked up Luna and slipped it under Mikey's arm, giving him a kiss. Stepping back to the door, she took one last look and whispered, "Goodnight, my little loves."

She stepped into her bedroom and stripped off her scrubs. Feeling the need for something special, she slipped a green silk negligee over her head and let the short skirt float around her thighs. The matching bikini panties rode low on her hips. She fluffed her hair as best she could, pinched her cheeks to add some color, and dabbed on a little lip gloss.

She stopped at the top of the stairs and listened for a moment to detect any sounds from the living room. Not hearing anything, she slowly walked down and turned into the living room. She gasped at the sight of the champagne, strawberries, and cannoli laid out picnic style. Conor's brawny arms wrapped around her waist and pulled her back against his chest.

"Ye look stunning, *ár ghrá*. The green of Shannon suits you. Come sit, and let us ply ye with sweets."

She turned around and looked up into Conor's beautiful aquamarine eyes. The flickering light from the fireplace created highlights and shadows on his cheekbones. She reached up on her tiptoes and wrapped her arms around his neck to kiss him. Flicking her tongue across the seam of his lips, he opened, and she slipped inside. She found he'd already had nibbled on at least one strawberry. A large warmth molded to her back, and Rick's lips caressed her shoulder. He slid the thin strap of her nightgown to the side, and his lips traveled up her shoulder and neck as he moved her hair aside. Separating from Conor's lips, she let them lead her over to the pillows they had set up in front of the fire.

"This is beautiful. I can't believe you two went to the trouble."

Conor propped against the sofa, and she nestled between his legs, leaning back against him. He lifted a flute of champagne and handed it to her. She took a small sip, and fruity bubbles danced across her taste buds. She'd never had such delicious champagne before. The taste was light and crisp. She could see herself imbibing too much and losing her head.

"It's never trouble to make you feel special, angel. We know things have been stressful lately, and we wanted to pamper you. Close your eyes." Rick reached down and picked up a strawberry. "Open those luscious lips for us."

Calleigh opened, and the tip of a strawberry rolled against her lower lip. She took a bite out of the succulent fruit. The combination of flavors made her moan. Conor's hands caressed her belly in circles. His lips occasionally landed on her neck. She opened her eyes when his deep voice whispered in her ear.

"Keep them closed, *muirnín*."

She felt the edge of the flute at her lips and let them slip more of the cool drink in her mouth, letting the bubbles linger on her tongue before swallowing. Next, she felt something else on her lips. It wasn't a strawberry, so it must be the cannoli. Slipping her tongue out, she took a little lick at the end of the roll and heard twin groans. Opening her mouth, she let Rick feed her a bite of the dessert. The crisp dough and sweet filling filled her mouth. She leaned her head back on Conor's chest and enjoyed the delicacy.

Moments later, they placed another strawberry at her lips, and after she took a bite, she felt Conor's tongue flick across her lips to taste the lingering juice. Her eyes were still closed when his hand slid up from her belly to hold her chest against him. Rick must have scooted closer because he spread her legs and wrapped them around his lean waist and hips. Hands crept up her legs to rest on her thighs. Expecting them to go higher, she let out a little whimper when they stopped their travels.

Conor and Rick lifted her hands and linked their fingers together. Rick's hand was soft in her grasp while Conor's felt damp. She felt Conor's lips next to her ear, his warm breath caressing her cheek.

"*Ár teaghlach churthaigh sibh.*"

"We created our family."

"*Luchtaíonn sibh grá, bríoghas, agus greann ár laethanta.*"

"Love, passion, and humor fill our days."

"*Coinníonn tú i gcónaí ár croí.*"

"You hold our hearts forever."

Calleigh's heart raced. Her breath catching as the words sank in. The living room vanished for a moment, and she could only focus on her men's voices.

"*Slánaigh tú ár anam.*"

"You complete our souls."

"*An mbeidh tú mar chéile agam?*"

"Will you be our wife?"

Her eyes flew open with the last phrase, and she looked down. Conor slid a ring on her left ring finger. Tears gathered in her eyes as she stared at the artistry of the jewelry, the symbol of their love a solid weight on her hand. She turned her hand back and forth and side to side, watching the firelight dance across the silver band and clear stone.

"Angel?"

She realized she hadn't answered them. "Of course, I'll marry you. But how..."

"We discussed logistics. If you're agreeable, we decided you would legally marry Conor. He's both an American and Irish citizen, so any future children we have would be eligible for dual status. The boys are a little trickier, but it wouldn't be any hardship to get them passports and such for when we want to visit Conor's mom and dad. We were thinking we'd have a private ceremony on Cape Cod with close friends and family shortly after, uniting the three of us."

She held her arms out for Rick. He moved in, braced his hands on the sofa, and leaned to kiss her. Their lips met to seal their intentions. When Rick pulled away, she tilted her head back and raised her chin to accept Conor's kiss. His erection pushed into her lower back, and she wanted to feel him inside her again.

She pulled back from his lips and wiggled out of the sandwich. Standing with the fire to her back, she reached down and pulled the nightgown over her head, baring her body to her loves. Rick came forward and slid the silky underwear down her hips. She lifted her feet to step out of the material and accepted Rick's hand to help her kneel back on the nest they'd built on the floor. Rick kneeled in front of her and slid a hand down the center of her body to between her legs. Conor moved behind her and reached a hand around to caress one of her nipples. Her breasts swelled in response. She closed her eyes and reveled in the sensations of their hands moving across her body. It no longer matter which hand belonged to whom.

Lips nuzzled her neck and breasts. Conor gathered her into his chest when Rick leaned back to undress. When his magnificent body was on display, he kneeled back down in front of her and captured her so Conor could do the same. He kissed her as his hands traveled down the length of her spine to cup her ass. His erection was hot and hard against her skin. They guided her back, so she was lying amongst the pillows. They lowered their heads, and both mouths latched onto a nipple, tugging and licking in different rhythms. Rick drew hard as Conor gave a soft lick. The dichotomy sent spirals of desire racing through her body. Her clit swelled, begging for a touch.

"Oh, my God..." she whimpered into the fire-lit room. Her hips surged upwards to let them know what she needed.

Rick and Conor slid a hand down her torso. One stopped at her clit and rubbed on the pulsing nerves, while the other dipped his broad finger inside. Calleigh spread her legs to give them more room as she pushed against their hands. Their long fingers alternated. One sliding deep, while the other tormented her bud. She felt her orgasm climbing. Writhing on the blankets, she reached for her climax but became frustrated as it seemed elusive.

"Don't fight for it, angel. Trust us to take care of you."

She tried to clear her mind of all but the feel of them inside her body. Their lips were at her breasts, their fingers probing deep inside to massage her swollen damp tissues. Their tongues flicking across her skin and their teeth nibbling on tender flesh. The wave crested again, and this time she allowed them to carry her over. The pulsing climax rolled through her body. When she surfaced, Conor was between her legs. He gently spread her open and licked across her wet folds.

"Hmmm ... it's been too long since I tasted ye. Yer a drug te me senses."

His nimble tongue good for more than just whispered wicked words and lyrical seductions. Long licks up and down the folds had her arching her hips to get closer. The tip of his tongue tormented the opening of her pussy, but never entered. He swirled around her clit, before his lips latched on and sucked. She cried out and surged forward, desperately needing something inside her.

She opened her eyes to see Rick holding his cock like an offering. Angling her head, she licked at the weeping head and relished his hiss. Trying to take him inside her mouth, she couldn't get around him at her current angle. He must have sensed her frustration because he moved to kneel over her head and slowly fed his length down her throat as Conor simultaneously pushed two fingers inside her. Her cries vibrated around Rick's flesh. Rick was bent over her body and leaned down to flatten his tongue on her clit, while Conor thrust deep inside her pussy. Their heads were so close they could have kissed each other. It would only take a slip of someone's tongue. She redoubled her efforts on Rick's cock, reaching her hands up to pull on his ass and trying to signal for him to let go and fuck her. His hips surged, and he drove inside over and over. She felt him get harder and his cock pulsed, but just before she was sure he was going to climax, he pulled away and swung around on the side of her.

Rick laid down on his back. "We're going to do this a little differently, angel. I want you to lie on me but face up to Conor."

Calleigh settled over the top of his body. The soft hair on his chest tickled her skin. Rick grasped her hips to hold her in place. Calleigh knew he wouldn't let her slip off, but she couldn't quite figure out exactly what they had in mind. Conor kneeled in front of her and spread her legs.

"Now stay here and relax while Conor gets you ready, love."

Conor picked up the tube of lube, clicked open the cap and squeezed out a liberal amount onto his fingers. Rick held her still while Conor put his fingers to the closed rosette of her ass and pushed his way through the ring to stretch her opening. She loved the slight burn and stretch while her men prepared her body for their love. Rick's cock was so hard against her ass.

Conor held up the bottle of lube with a question in his eyes. Calleigh felt Rick nod. She knew her eyes widened when Conor's large hand surrounded Rick's cock to slick it up. She'd never seen them touch each other before in a sexual way, but from the sound of Rick's moan beneath them, her fiancé's grip was pleasurable.

Calleigh studied Conor to see how he reacted to the intimate touch of his best friend. There didn't seem to be anything other than the now familiar signs of arousal on the Irishman. Conor nodded and Calleigh knew she was about to fly. Rick lifted Calleigh's hips and guided his cock deep inside her ass. Instead of thrusting, Rick held her still, stuffed full of cock. Calleigh needed him to move. She ached for each driving plunge of her lovers' cocks. She opened her mouth to beg when Conor came down over the top of her. He fit his cock to Calleigh's pussy.

Being filled by both her men was a feeling she could never eloquently describe. Their bodies joined, their breaths mingling, their skin sealed together as they moved as one. Conor thrust up, the head of his cock rubbing against that spot inside that drove her crazy, as Rick pulled back. Their countering thrusts made sure her body was never empty. Conor grabbed the back of her head and slammed their lips together. His tongue drove into her mouth in the same tempo of his cock. Rick's hands separated her cheeks as he drove forcefully deep inside her body. Groans and cries echoed throughout the room.

Their strokes became less rhythmic as they neared orgasm, their hips jerking, her straining into every thrust, milking out each sensation. Calleigh screamed into Conor's mouth as a tremendous orgasm ripped through her body. She felt every tissue in her pussy and ass contract around the thick shafts buried deep inside her. She ripped away from Conor, desperate to fill her lungs with air. Rick and Conor both slammed into her one last time and held deep. Their cocks pulsed as they released their seed deep inside her body.

# Chapter Ten

♥

C alleigh opened the door to the ladies' room and ran smack into Carla. It took a moment for her eyes to focus on the swimming letters of her friend's scrub shirt.

"That's it. I'm taking you to see someone." Carla grabbed Calleigh's hand and pulled her down the hall.

"Carla, stop! What are you doing?" She pulled her hand from her friend's firm grip.

"I heard you throwing up again. You swear up and down that you're not pregnant, but this is not going away. So we're going to find out exactly what is going on." Carla picked up Calleigh's hand again and tugged.

"I'm fine. I told you that. Look, maybe I picked up a little virus or something. It's winter. In Boston. We work in a hospital and there is a satan's spawn strain of Influenza A going around. I promise to take it easy this weekend."

"You swe—"

Calleigh bolted for the bathroom stall again. The door came back and smacked her on the side as she bent over the toilet, bracing her hand on the automatic flushing sensor as her empty stomach heaved clear bile into the bowl.

"That's it. If you don't listen to me, I'm calling reinforcements. Hey, Miranda. Is Vic or Chase on duty right now? Vic is? Great, can you call him and ask him to meet Calleigh and I in the pit? Yes, she's still getting sick. I know, that's what I told her. No, of course she's not being reasonable. Yes, you may need the padded restraints."

Calleigh would have laughed if she wasn't so utterly miserable. Not to mention in need of some clean scrubs. Tops and bottoms.

"Carla ... I give in. But will you at least save a portion of my dignity by grabbing me a fresh pair of scrubs from the dispenser before I have to face the pit crew and my friends?"

"Of course. Did you miss the bowl?"

"No, but I've given birth to twins and the pleasure of womanhood post childbirth is less pelvic floor control under stress and I've been heaving my guts out."

"Ah, got it."

"Wait!"

"Yeah?"

"How did you know about Miranda's husbands?"

Carla leaned against the wall while Calleigh washed her mouth out ... again. Her friend had a smirky grin and rolled her eyes.

"Gabby goes to the same daycare as my nephew. I pick him up sometimes, and occasionally run into either of her dads or Miranda."

"Is that why you were so nonchalant when I introduced you to Rick and Conor?"

Carla pushed off the wall and rubbed Calleigh's back. "No, sweetie. My sister and brother-in-law have shared an open marriage for almost thirty years. They both bring additional partners to my dinner parties regularly. It's never mattered to me who someone loves, as long as all involved are consenting and honest about their relationship."

Calleigh leaned against Carla. "If I could express a deep thought or emotion beyond misery right now, I would gladly share it with you."

"Let me get you some clean scrubs, then we'll have Vic check you out."

One change of clothes and a new definition to the walk of shame found Calleigh herded into the pit and plopped on a gurney. She spied Vic as he pushed his way through the doors and looked around. As one of the program directors, he rarely found himself in the ER and Calleigh grinned as he used his charm to cajole a nurse into giving him the lay of the land. Clearly, it worked because Vic smiled and headed in Calleigh's direction.

"Hey, Calleigh. What's the problem? Miranda said you needed help."

"She's been throwing up and has a loss of appetite. She swears up and down she's not pregnant. Oh, and she's not been sleeping through the night for the past three weeks." Carla reported.

Calleigh turned to Carla in shock. "How do you know that?"

Carla faced her best friend and took hold of her hand. "I called Rick and Conor a week or so ago, and they told me."

Calleigh yanked her hand out of Carla's grasp. "Why are you calling them behind my back!"

"Because I'm worried about you! Now stop being so stubborn. I know you're all about self-reliance, but you can't keep putting yourself at risk to spare the feelings or make life easier on those around you." She faced Vic again. "Please? Just do a basic exam?"

Vic nodded. "Sorry Calleigh. I agree with Carla. What makes you think you're not pregnant? Both my wife and husband are horrible gossips, so I know you have a healthy sex life."

"For multiple reasons. Number one, I take the Depo shot and have for years. My last shot was approximately two and a half months ago.

Two, I had a period approximately a month ago. Granted, it was light, but that's not unusual for me since starting the shot after the boys were born. Finally, three, I'm not throwing up every morning or after I eat. It's just random. I've been under a lot of stress. Miles has been stirring up trouble with the administration, although I think that's settled now, and my mother-in-law is threatening to sue for custody of my children because she doesn't approve of my fiancées."

"Okay, I agree there's some stress there. Any number of things can cause your symptoms. We'll run a CBC panel and I'll do a quick physical. You have a primary care, right?"

"Umm ... sort of? I mean, I guess I do, but haven't been in like five years. I get my annual well woman from my OBGYN and call it a day." Vic frowned and Carla gasped. "So I guess it's time to make an appointment?" Both of her friends nodded their heads. "Fine."

Vic called over a nurse, his voice a mix of urgency and curiosity, and asked where he could find a blood draw kit. The sterile scent of antiseptic hung in the air as he walked away, his footsteps disappearing into the chaos of the packed emergency room. Calleigh trailed her fingers over the cool, smooth surface of her engagement ring. The diamond caught the harsh glow of the fluorescent lights, scattering a delicate spectrum of light across the room. She couldn't suppress the soft smile that tugged at her lips, her heart warming at the vivid memory of her fiancées' tender proposal.

"Hey Calleigh!"

She looked up and saw a nurse standing near the elevators. She thought the woman'd name was Melissa, but couldn't be sure. "Yes?"

She waved her over. Calleigh looked at Carla. "I'll be right back."

She hopped down from the gurney and walked over. Behind Melissa stood a delivery man with a bunch of flowers. Her heart flipped over at the idea that maybe Conor and Rick had sent her some. In the two weeks since their proposal, they'd left little love notes all over the house for her to find. Her favorite was the other morning when she stepped out of the shower to find one of them had written *Wish we were here* on the mirror in soap, so it appeared in the steam.

"What's up?"

"This guy was looking for you up in surgery. I ran into Carla in the locker room and knew you were down here. Is everything okay?"

"I'm fine. Just a precautionary check-up. You know, with everything going around?"

"Ugh, don't get me started. My kid got that flu bug last week. 103 fever for six days straight. Hope you're all good. The surgery schedule is crazy right now, and you're the best anesthetist we've got."

Melissa jabbed the button to go back up to the surgical floor and, in a minor miracle, the doors opened right away. As soon as she was gone, Calleigh turned to the delivery guy. "Can I help you?"

"Are you Calleigh Wells?"

She looked at the pretty flowers and inhaled, trying to catch their scent. "Yes. Are those for me?"

"Yes." He handed her a clipboard. "I just need you to sign, please."

She accepted the pen and signed on the line next to her printed name. When she looked up, the man had taken off his delivery hat and held out a piece of paper.

"You've been served. Have a nice day."

Calleigh watched as he walked past, the sound of the sliding doors echoing behind him as he left the department. When she looked down, the word "subpoena," stark and ominous in big, bold letters, jumped out at her. Her hands trembled, the paper crinkling like dry leaves, as she opened the document. Calleigh scanned the first few lines, then a guttural scream tore from her throat. Darkness consumed her, pressing down with the weight of a thousand shattered dreams.

"Calleigh? Come on girl, wake up."

Muddled senses caused her to peel her eyes open. After she blinked several times, the room came into focus. Her brain tried to remember what had happened, and suddenly awareness snapped. She bolted upright and grabbed the railing on the side of the bed as her head swam for a few seconds. She laid on a gurney in one of the curtained-off exam areas. Vic and Carla stood beside the bed, the expressions of concern mirrored on their faces.

She fell back onto the bed and flung an arm up to cover her eyes from the bright fluorescent lights overhead. "What happened?"

"You passed out," Vic responded. He nodded to the packet of papers at the foot of the bed. "I'm guessing what's in there came as a shock. When you came to a moment later, you started crying hysterically and yelling for Rick and Conor, so I gave you a sedative."

"Oh my God," she moaned.

How embarrassing that she acted that way in her place of work, but she couldn't stop the tears from filling her eyes as she looked over at Carla. Calleigh hadn't gone into detail with Carla about the problems with her former mother-in-law. She wished Miranda were here, but she and Chase were in surgery upstairs. "She's trying to take my babies away. Rick swears it won't happen, but what if he's mistaken? What if his lawyer friend didn't get it right? If I lost Rick and Conor, my heart would shatter all over again, but if I lose my babies, I just might die."

"Calleigh, I don't want to sound condescending or anything, but as your doctor, at the moment, I need you to breathe and remain calm."

She took a few deep breaths at Vic's words. God bless him, he was always so nice.

"Good. Now, if Rick trusts this lawyer he talked to, then I'm sure nothing bad will happen. She's trying to stir up trouble. Besides, you shouldn't get overly upset. It's not good for the baby." Vic's lips twitched, trying to keep a straight face.

"How do you know it won't happen? You can't guarantee ... What do you mean 'baby'?"

*Did I hear that right? It's not possible.*

Vic picked up Calleigh's hand. "You *are* pregnant, Calleigh. I ran a blood test while you were unconscious. I know I'm not an OB or anything, but I am pretty good at imaging. So, I did an ultrasound to confirm because of the bleeding you reported. I suspect the bleeding occurred at the time of implantation."

She couldn't wrap her mind around it. She'd taken the shot. Granted, she and her lovers had used no form of protection, but what were the odds that the Depo shot would fail? One and a half percent ... maybe? "But what about the shot?"

"Well, I looked up your electronic records, and they showed you receiving a flu shot back in September, but nothing about your Depo."

She shook her head. "That can't be right. I declined the flu shot. They asked me that same day, but I said no. Told them to just do the other."

"Regardless of how it happened, you are pregnant. I recommend you schedule an appointment with your obstetrician to confirm, but my estimate puts you around eight weeks."

"Oh my God," she whispered right when Rick and Conor came running into the curtained area.

Rick rushed to the bed where Calleigh lay. "Angel? What happened?" He cupped her cheek and placed a soft kiss on her cool lips. "You're so pale. My heart nearly stopped when Carla called and said you passed out, then started screaming for us."

"Aye, he came barging into my office like his ass was on fire, *Muirnín*. It's a miracle we dinna get stopped by the Gardi the way we gave it a good foot through this city to get here."

She held Conor's hand on one side of the bed and Rick's on the other. "I don't remember what happened after I woke up. They told me I went into hysterics. Loves, she served me papers. Susan actually filed a dispute of custody."

"That unholy bitch! I never thought the woman would actually go so far. How dare she disrupt our home? How dare she hurt you this way? There is no better mother than my angel. Your love for those boys is stamped into every action of every day."

"*Go n-ithe an cat thú, is go n-ithe an diabhal an cat,*" Conor spat under his breath.

"Um, Con? Did you just put a hex on the woman? Can you teach me one?" Rick tried to lighten the tension.

"Sorry. I said 'may the cat eat ye and the devil eat the cat'. 'Tis an auld family curse."

Calleigh smiled. "I like that one. One thing about the Irish is that you're very creative with your cursing. Give me a kiss and whisper sweet nothings in my ear."

The tender pressure of Conor's lips, the taste of him, the feeling of his love — Calleigh closed her eyes to absorb it all. Each kiss from Conor was a unique story, told through the pressure of his lips and the warmth of his breath. Tales of dark seduction whispered on the wind, mingled with bursts of laughter, and finally, a warm embrace, like a sunbeam, soothed her troubled soul.

"Calleigh, I think we need to face this head on. Why don't we contact Susan? Tell her to come over to the house to discuss this idiocy. If we drag lawyers into this, it's going to turn into a nightmare. Why don't we try talking it out with her first?" Rick asked.

"I'll try, but you saw her that night. There was no talking to her rationally. For now, I have to get back to work. I'll meet you at home later."

"Oh no, you are not, missy," Carla scolded.

"Carla! Have you been listening this whole time?"

She poked her head through the curtain. "Sue me. You *are* going home. You *are* going to bed. And you will call me and tell me *everything*." She gave Calleigh a pointed look.

"Angel? Is there something you're not telling us? Something else? Did I see Vic down here? Where did *he*, go?"

Calleigh twisted the sheets on the bed between her fingers. "Um ... well... the thing is..."

"'Tis okay, *mo ghrá*. Ye can tell us. This is about ye still gettin' sick, isn't it?" He saw the shocked look on Calleigh's face. "Aye love, we knew. We dinna say anythin' cos we wanted ye te come te us. Please tell us. What's wrong?"

She took a deep breath. "Apparently, I'm pregnant. Somebody screwed up. I never got my shot, and Vic thinks I'm about eight weeks along." She rushed it all out in one breath.

Rick plopped down on the bed next to Calleigh's legs. He pulled her up into his embrace. She latched onto him. Her eyes turned into spigots and soaked Rick's shirt. Warmth surrounded her when Conor molded himself to her back and encircled her waist.

"Angel, those had better be happy tears. This is the best thing we've ever heard—next to you agreeing to marry us anyway."

She pulled her head up off Rick's shoulder. "Really? You're not upset? I didn't know if you were ready for something like this. I know it's shocked the hell out of me."

"We're havin' a babby. 'Tis a blessin' to celebrate." Conor held Calleigh's face between his hands and kissed her. Their lips welded together as he wiped the tears from her cheeks.

"Let's go home. We have to plan how to tell the boys to expect a little brother or sister. I think we should make it a game." Rick rubbed his hands together as plots started forming in his mind. Scooping Calleigh up off the bed, he carried her out of the hospital to her embarrassment and the cheers of her co-workers.

# Chapter Eleven

♥

C onor paced around the living room. He looked up at the clock on the mantel and grimaced. *It couldn't possibly be two minutes since he last looked.* He turned his back to the clock and walked to the bow windows to peek between the curtains.

"Con, stop pacing. She'll get here when she gets here. No matter how fast you turn in circles, time doesn't actually speed up."

"Ask me bollocks. I just wanna get this over with. I'm afraid the *bitseach* is goin' te make this as difficult as possible. Calleigh disna need any more stress."

They took a week to persuade Susan to see them after Calleigh received the papers. He and Rick had bombarded her with calls and messages. At first, she had refused to talk to them at all, telling them to contact her lawyer. When Calleigh tried, she spent twenty minutes on the phone, half the time holding the receiver away from her ear as Susan harangued her. She'd finally gotten fed up and yelled for Susan to shut her mouth. She'd told Susan unless she wanted the tape recording of the conversation to make its way into her lawyer's hands, she would meet with them.

The doorbell rang, and Conor jumped forward to open the door. Rick's hand landed on his shoulder to stop him.

"Make her wait. Don't appear too anxious or aggressive."

Conor took a deep breath and attempted to calm his racing heart. He knew Rick was right. This was not an occasion to let his Irish temper get the best of him. Turning his head, he looked at the stairway. Calleigh had paused on the middle step. Her face was pale and her eyes filled with anxiety. He forgot the door and walked up the few steps separating them.

"It 'ill be gran', *Muirnín*. We'll sit down an' talk this out like rational adults." He placed his hand on her flat belly where their child nested. "How is *ár caragan*? The little darling is not giving you any trouble today?"

She placed her hand over his. "We're good." She looked over Conor's shoulder at Rick standing by the front door. "Let her in." She cupped Conor's cheek. "Once you're in the living room, I'll bring the boys down to the playroom and get them settled."

Rick opened the door and saw Susan on the front stoop, but she wasn't alone. He held the door wider to allow them to enter. One by one, they filed through, and he accepted their coats.

"This is my lawyer, Mr. Nielson, and Ms. Waterman from the Department of Children and Families. I brought them so they can see for themselves what is occurring in this house."

Conor couldn't believe Susan's audacity. "We invited you here to discuss your concerns as a family. We did not authorize you to bring anyone else into our home."

He saw the surprised looks on the faces of the lawyer and social worker. It appeared Susan had given them some misinformation.

She pointed her finger at the man before her. "That's precisely why I wanted them here. So they could see just what this place is like when you haven't coached Kevin's children about what to say." She looked around. "Where are my grandchildren? I demand to see them."

Calleigh stepped forward, so she was face-to-face with her mother-in-law. "Our sons are just getting up from their nap. We will give them their snack, then they will go to the playroom while we speak. If, after getting to know Ms. Waterman, we are agreeable, she may speak with them, but *you* will not until I am assured you can control the venomous words from spewing out of your mouth."

Conor guided the three interlopers into the living room after Calleigh and Rick went upstairs to collect Mikey and Bran. "Canna I offer ye something to drink?"

"I would love a coffee if you have it ready, and please call me John," Nielson responded, settling into the club chair near the windows.

"Make that two please, and you may call me Jamie," Ms. Waterman answered. Conor nodded his head in acknowledgement. "Susan?"

All he got in return was a haughty stare as she sat primly on the sofa.

"In that case ... Calleigh and Rick will be down in a moment after they've gotten the boys settled. I'll have yer cuppa ready shortly."

He walked through the archway into the kitchen. Grabbing two mugs from the cabinet, he attempted to release some of the rage boiling through him. The addition of the officials recast this meeting. He knew he shouldn't become defensive, but family threats spurred an instinctive reaction. He placed the mugs, sweetener, and milk on a tray, then carried it back into the living room.

He handed the two officials their coffee. "As I said earlier, we invited Susan here te discuss her concerns. We respect her as Mikey and Brandon's *seanmháthair*," he looked at her, "but we want to make sure ye understand that we are their parents and will make decisions regarding their upbringing."

"That is exactly why I've filed the suit. People like you have no business raising children. You perverts will poison their minds and give them no moral code."

Calleigh entered the room, catching that last statement. "And I suppose you believe being raised in a house where you preach hate and bigotry is a more nurturing environment?"

"It is not wrong to teach a child morality based on Christian values. I did so with Kevin, and he grew into an upstanding man who became a national hero."

Calleigh nodded her head. "Yes, he did. He also understood and accepted alternative lifestyles. Our marriage was a direct reflection of that."

Rick stood next to the mantel and addressed the room. "Our argument with you has nothing to do with Kevin's character. It's truly a tragedy that he never had the opportunity to raise his sons. I'm sure he would have made a brilliant father, but that is neither here nor now."

Conor held up his hand to halt the conversation. "'Tis obvious we dinna agree on certain aspect of our lives. Ye may not approve of our lifestyle, but what I don't understan' is why that entitles ye te involve the legal system in a custody dispute."

"Let me take this," Jamie responded. "At DCF, we were told—and John was told the same thing—that Mrs. Wells feared for the safety of her grandchildren. She reported possible abuse of a sexual nature."

Conor couldn't breathe. He knew Susan disapproved, but he'd did not know she would tell blatant lies to get her way.

"That is the most preposterous accusation I've ever heard! I would never put my children in jeopardy!" Calleigh yelled.

Susan stood up and got in Calleigh's face. "How do we know you're not forcing my grandchildren to watch or even participate in the sexual orgies that no doubt occur in this den of depravity?"

"Susan, sit down. Now," John said from the corner of the room.

Conor approved of the steel hardness in the attorney's voice despite his so far exhibited quiet nature. Obviously, he was fed up with the whole proceeding; this eased a knot in Conor's gut. Conor went to stand next to Rick at the fireplace. He needed Rick's steadfastness with the emotions swirling throughout the room.

"Again, that supposition goes back to your opinion of our lifestyle. There is no evidence of physical, sexual or emotional abuse in our home," Rick said.

Jamie set her coffee cup down on the tray and stood. "Mr. Connor, Mr. McGuire, Calleigh, I believe I've heard enough of this conversation. Would you be agreeable to me speaking with Michael and Brandon so I can make a complete report?"

Conor thought the idea had merit. If she spoke with the boys, he was certain any lingering questions would be put to rest. He looked at Rick and Calleigh to determine how they responded to the request and saw them give a slight nod. "I believe tha' would be acceptable, provided one of us supervises." He again looked to Rick and Calleigh. "Rick?"

Conor watched the social worker and Rick walk back to the playroom. He was ready for this evening to be over and he knew his m*uirnín* needed it to be, too. The sleepless nights and stress were catching up to her. Most likely, the pregnancy contributed to her lack of energy as well. He noticed her wilting and went to sit next to her on the sofa, and she leaned against him. He slipped his arm around her shoulder and placed a soft kiss on her temple, pulling her in closer to his side.

Susan gave her a dirty look from the chair across the room.

"Calleigh, I notice the ring on your finger. Are you planning to remarry?" Susan asked.

Calleigh looked down at the ring. "Yes, we are planning a spring wedding on the Cape."

Conor lifted her left hand, his thumb brushing against her skin as he kissed the ring that he and Rick had placed there. He'd spent countless hours in the jeweler's workshop, poring over sketches and metal samples, to create a custom piece that not only symbolized their bond as a trio but captured Calleigh's vibrant spirit. The scent of polishing compounds and the soft glow of the jeweler's lamp were ingrained in his memory. He desired *a ghrá* to proudly display the symbol of their love.

Susan leaned forward. "I notice you have quite an accent, Mr. McGuire. May I ask if you have a current visa?"

Conor rolled his eyes. "Naw, I don' require one."

"Why ever not? Did you manage to complete the naturalization process?"

"Actually, I'm a natural-born citizen. Me da is a retired colonel in the United States Air Force. Me ma is Irish, and I lived in Ireland most of me life, with the exceptions of summers in England during me da's posting. I moved here te attend university an' decided te stay."

"Oh, I see."

Conor heard a cough from the corner as the attorney tried to disguise a chuckle. A knock sounded, causing Conor to squeeze Calleigh's shoulder before he stood to answer. When he opened the door, he found Calleigh's mom. "Hiya Lilly, tis nice te see ye. We're havin' a bit of company, won't ye join us?"

Lilly gave Conor a hug and whispered in his ear, "I came for moral support. How's she doing?"

Conor didn't want Susan or the lawyer to overhear his true opinion on the matter, so he just gave Lilly a look.

"That good, huh?"

They made their way into the living room.

Calleigh stood and walked around the edge of the sofa. "Mom. So glad to see you." She gave her a big hug. "This is John Nielson, Susan's attorney. And I'm sure you remember Susan, Kevin's mother."

Lilly nodded her head in acknowledgement. "Susan. Can't say it's nice to see you under these circumstances."

Lilly didn't even try to disguise her anger at the other woman. Calleigh backed away, and Conor pulled her into a backwards hug as he propped himself on the wall.

"Lilly, I don't understand how you can condone this situation. Michael and Brandon are your grandchildren, too. What happens in this house is—"

"Stop right there. I have no problem with Calleigh's relationship with Conor and Rick because I've seen them interact with each other on nearly a daily basis for the last three years. Did you know they were the ones who brought her home the day she found out about Kevin? It was their arms that held her as her heart tore in two. They were the ones who stood beside her, helped her with the boys when they were still infants, made her smile again. They healed her heart, and she stole theirs. I know how much they love Calleigh and Michael and Brandon. They would give their lives for them, and that is all I need to know. I don't care what occurs in their bedroom. Frankly, it's none of our business."

Conor heard footsteps and saw Rick and Jamie enter the living room at that moment. He released Calleigh and turned to face the group.

Rick held the boys' hands, and they stopped in front of Susan.

Susan sat down and tried to pull her grandchildren into her arms, but they stepped away. "Michael? Brandon? Why don't you give grandma a hug?"

"Why you take us away?" Mikey asked.

Susan scowled at Rick. "Sweeties. I just want to make sure that you grow up to be like your daddy. Big, strong, happy, good men."

"Wick is our daddy. Conna is our da. They are big," Brandon replied.

Susan shook her head. "They may be big, but I'm afraid of what they are teaching you. They may be bad men."

Mikey scratched his head. "Conna teach us to bike."

"They just got tricycles. They're learning how to pedal on their own," Rick explained.

Brandon nodded his head in agreement. "Wick make smiley takes. Bad man no make smiley takes."

"The boys' favorite Sunday breakfast is smiley pancakes," Calleigh clarified.

"They kiss our boo-boos." Mikey pointed out the band-aid on his knee.

"They read stories." Brandon held out a book to show his grandma, then walked over and gave it to Conor. "This one."

Conor lifted Brandon in his arms and accepted the book. "Ye bet, *mo grian*." He kissed him on the forehead, then put him down. "Go give *mamó* a hug."

As Brandon ran and hugged Lilly, Conor noticed the glistening tears in Calleigh's eyes, hearing the soft sniffles that accompanied them. The boys' innocent, earnest defense of him and Rick pulled at his heartstrings. Calleigh put a hand to her stomach and rubbed their unborn child. Conor winked at her, a silent message passing between them. He knew Calleigh had been nervous about his and Rick's reaction to her pregnancy, but Conor absolutely loved stepping in as Mikey and Brandon's da, and he couldn't wait to hold their baby in his arms. Calleigh had apologized to both of them earlier in the week, but there was nothing to forgive.

Calleigh went over and stood beside Rick. He pulled her into an embrace as she looked down at Susan, sitting in the chair with a stunned look on her face as Mikey turned around and joined his brother at Lilly's side.

"Susan. I will fight you to the death to keep my family intact, but I ask you to drop this ridiculous suit. It will only lead to heartache on both sides. I think we've shown you here tonight that, although we may be a unique family, we have all the love and nurturing abilities of a traditional home. If anything, there is more to go around."

Susan stood and walked to the closet to retrieve her coat. "I will never approve of what you've turned into, Calleigh Wells. In fact, I'm ashamed to call you my daughter-in-law, but I will not hurt my grandchildren, and they have the misguided notion these men are their dads. I dearly hope you don't come to regret your actions as they grow into adults and learn just what you are. When they ask questions about their real father, please send me notice." She walked out the door.

Conor couldn't believe, after all of Susan's pontificating on family values that she'd turn her back on Michael and Brandon without even saying goodbye. He shook his head in regret.

Nielson stood from the chair where he'd taken residence and addressed the room. "Calleigh, Rick, Conor, I wish to apologize to you. Had I known this was a witch hunt, I never would have agreed to represent Mrs. Wells. It's obvious to me this is the perfect home for your sons. In fact, I hope my partner and I are as successful at parenting as you three have become. You see, we recently adopted a little boy a year younger than Michael and Brandon." He smiled.

Calleigh laughed. "Don't give us too much credit. Most days we're making things up as we go."

"I, too, will file my report and officially close this file. You have my respect for the way you handled this situation," Jamie said.

Calleigh showed both of them out. The moment she shut the door, Conor wrapped his arms around her, and placed a kiss on the back of her neck.

"Ye see, *mo ghrá,* everything has worked out. I'm sorry the boys willna have their other grandma in their lives, but I think there's enough of us te make up for the loss."

"That's just it, Conor. I feel that not having her in their lives is no loss, and that makes me sad because on one level she has a point. She raised Kevin, and he was an amazing man. He would have been a terrific father. With her reactions, she's denying them the relationship with that half of their family."

She stepped away from the door and turned to face everyone in the room. Rick came over and held her between him and Conor. She raised her head and received a kiss.

"That's her choice, angel. You aren't denying them. She is. Kevin would understand that. I don't think he would find fault with you."

She leaned her head on Rick's chest for another minute, then stepped away. Kneeling down, she held out her arms, and both boys ran to her. "My little loves, mommy is so proud of you. You said very nice things about your daddies." She wiped away the errant tear that slid down her cheek. "Now how about we get some dinner then we all have movie night?" She looked up at her mom. "Are you going to join us?"

"I would love to, but I promised your father I'd bring home takeout from *Mirabelle's.*"

Calleigh stood and gave her mom another hug. "Thank you for coming. For saying what you did."

"I only speak the truth. Now, have a relaxing night with your family. I'll see you all this weekend. How about we all go to the aquarium? You want to go see the big fish and turtles, boys?"

Conor smiled as their eyes lit up and their twin heads nodded in unison. They loved the aquarium. They all said goodbye, and the group headed into the living room.

"Mikey and Brandon, you pick the movie tonight. Daddy can help you with the names. Da and I will get dinner started." Calleigh said.

# Epilogue

♥

Calleigh rested her head in Conor's lap while they streamed the most recent blockbuster. Out of the corner of her eye, she saw him playing with his wedding ring. Conor stroked her head. She sighed as he smoothed his hand up and down, lifting the tail end of her shirt to caress her lower back. Calleigh turned her head and nuzzled his crotch, rubbing her face against him like a cat. She played with his thickening shaft. She put enough pressure behind the movement to drive her husband to distraction.

"*Muirnín*, yer playin' with fire."

The material of his jeans dampened as her pink tongue traced the ridges of his erection. She knew by Conor's tense muscles he was moments away from unzipping and begging her to swallow his cock. Which she was more than happy to do.

"Sorry, Con. Someone else needs Calleigh's special skills right now."

Rick transferred baby Alannah Nicole into her arms. Conor pulled Calleigh between his legs to support her back. She loved sitting in her husband's embrace while they looked down when their child nursed. Calleigh caressed the tiny, rose-colored lips as they latched onto her nipple.

Rick sat next to Calleigh and Conor. "I know our interludes have been limited lately, but our daughter wanted food." He stroked Calleigh's legs and watch as her fingers smoothed the static flies of black hair on Alannah's tiny head.

Calleigh looked up at Rick. "Were the boys still asleep?"

"Out like lights. I think I actually wore them out today."

Rick and Conor had been out in the backyard of their new home, building the boys' first tree house. The boys' club had spent hours at work banging away at the boards. It wouldn't surprise Calleigh if at some point a sign saying 'no girls allowed' appeared on the structure.

The family moved to Roslindale and had found a wonderful home in a neighborhood surrounded by old-growth trees in the Metropolitan Hill area. The place had beautiful hardwood floors, French doors, and custom built-ins. But Rick, Conor, and Calleigh's favorite spot was sitting out on the deck late at night, listening to the crickets. For now, she was staying home with the kids, and Rick and Conor caught the commuter train daily. This was a peaceful neighborhood with all the advantages of being near the city they loved so much.

When Alannah signal she'd had enough, Calleigh lifted her to her shoulder and burped her. When she handed her back to Rick, he looked down into the sapphire-blue eyes that were wide open and staring at him.

"I'll go put her back to bed. Why don't the two of you head upstairs, and I'll meet you in our room shortly."

Calleigh proceeded Conor up the steps. His hands were on her hips the whole way. She had a surprise for her men tonight. She'd finally gotten the all clear from her doctor to make love again and was ready to experience the mind melting pleasure Rick and Conor always provided.

"You go ahead, and get in bed, love. I'm going to slip into the bathroom and wash up first." She gave him a hungry kiss and groped his reawakening crotch. "I'll take care of this when I get back."

He speared his hand through Calleigh's hair and captured her lips in a bruising kiss. "Dear God, I want ye Calleigh. I'm beggin' fer ye touch."

"Don't worry, I'll make sure you get what you need. Both of you."

She turned her back and sauntered into the master bath they'd renovated when they'd bought the house. She stripped from her clothes and, after pinning her hair up on top of her head, jumped in a quick shower. When she got out, she lathered her skin in lotion and slipped a sheer baby-doll nightie over her head. She left off the matching panties. When she peeked out the bathroom door, she saw Rick and Conor both in bed, with their eyes glued to the doorway. She opened the door and struck what she hoped looked like a sexy pose.

She guessed she achieved her purpose with the negligee because Rick and Conor were staring at her as if she were a feast and they were starving men. She knew the sheer fabric didn't conceal any of her attributes, and she gave them a sultry little smile.

"Heaven preserve us," Conor whispered.

"Uh-huh," Rick agreed.

Calleigh stepped onto the padded bench they had at the end of the bed. She stood looking down at her men. Slowly, she swayed her hips. She lifted her arms above her, while grasping the ribbon edged hem. She tilted her head and let her long hair drape down her back. Spreading her legs a little, she undulated to silent music. She heard the raspy breaths of Rick and Conor. Occasionally, a soft moan echoed in the room. She turned her back to them and bent at the knees, slowly straightening. Her right arm slid up her entire body as she arched her back to once again raise her hand over her head. She circled her hips like doing a rumba.

"Sweet God, have mercy on us," Rick agonizingly whispered.

Turning to face them again, she stepped over the footboard and stood with one foot between each man's spread legs. The light of the moon streaming through the skylight and large French doors leading to their small private deck overlooking the backyard broke the darkness of the room. In the muted light, she saw the fires blazing in her husbands' eyes.

Each man sat up and latched onto the leg in front of him. Conor's hand caressed up the front and Rick's up the back. Their lips and tongues played with the skin of her thighs. She reached down to grasp the hem of her nightie and dragged it up and over her head. When she looked down, both men stared up at her as if paying homage to their empress. She rested a hand on each of their cheeks, and they nuzzled into her palms.

"*Muirnín?*"

"I got the okay from my obstetrician this morning."

She stepped out from between their legs and kneeled on the bed. Rick's hand clasped hers and jerked her forward, only to catch her in his arms and lowered her onto her back. Her vision filled with his large, hard body leaning over her.

"Are there any restrictions, angel?"

"Well ... the doctor said we should go slow and not be surprised if it takes me a little time to enjoy ... everything, again. She also said we may need a little help in the moisture department." Calleigh knew she was blushing but hoped the dark room covered her embarrassment.

"Don't worry angel, we'll take things nice and slow. One touch at a time. One kiss. One slow, thoughtful flick of our tongues against your delectable body. Right Con?"

"Absolutely."

Conor rested his hand on her waist and slid up to cup her breast. Lifting the heavier mound, he caressed the tips. Calleigh closed her eyes and let out a sigh. Her breasts were more sensitive since she was nursing. Rick's finger dipped between her folds to play with her clit, rubbing back and forth, stimulating the bundle of nerves. Conor's head lowered and his lips claimed hers. She opened, and his tongue flicked against hers.

One of Rick's fingers circled in the opening of her pussy, dipping in only to pull back and circle hungry flesh some more.

"Please, Rick," she begged. She wanted to feel him inside her again.

He pushed the finger through again, embedding it fully inside her. She cried out as his touch sent sparks dancing along the awakening nerve endings. Rick added a second finger. Slowly, he stretched her. Conor licked at her breasts, occasionally flicking over the tips. She had already warned them about leakage, but neither of them complained about it. Rick removed his fingers, and she whimpered. He rolled her on top of him. She straddled his legs down by his knees.

"I think we should do it like this. So you can go at your own pace for now, angel."

"Put your hand out, *ár ghrá*." Conor put a dollop of lubrication in Calleigh's hand. "Now slick up his cock so it slides in real nice and easy."

Her hand wrapped around Rick's length and smoothed the cool gel up and down. He hissed, and his fingers dug into her hips. She pulled up and gave a little twist over the plum shaped head. Fluid flowed from the slit at the top.

"Angel, you'd better stop, or this will be over before we begin."

She scooted up so she could straddle his hips. Rick's hands were at her waist, and Conor's supported her hips. She eased down onto the long, thick cock waiting for her. Several minutes passed before he was fully inside her, but once their groins met, she sighed.

"Okay, *muirnín*, when you're ready, rise and take a few strokes. Let us know if you have any problems or if we need to change positions."

Rising to her knees, she felt every inch of Rick's cock still inside her as she descended. She was pleased there was no pain or discomfort. Doing so again, she let her weight carry her down harder. This time she cried out, but only because it felt so exquisite. Her fingertips dug into Rick's chest as she moved up and down. Closing her eyes, she concentrated on sensations. With each downward movement, his cock rubbed against her g-spot. She started moving up and down in shallow little strokes so the head kept sliding over it again and again.

Conor stilled Calleigh's strokes and leaned her forward to lie against Rick. She heard him pick up the bottle of lube and release some on his fingers. Conor smoothed the cool gel onto the skin surrounding her back entrance, then dipped a finger inside. Adding a second a few moments later. The stretch both foreign and familiar after the last several months of inactivity. But Calleigh's body welcomed her husband's touch and relaxed around the digits stretching her.

"Yer ready for me M*uirnín?*"

Calleigh nodded. Conor guided the head of his cock to her opening and slowly pushed forward. When the head popped through the ring of muscle, they both cried out.

"Gawd all fecking mighty, yer so hot and tight around me." He eased his entire length in.

Calleigh panted against Rick's neck the entire time. Conor and Rick began to move. She felt their cocks rubbing together through the thin membrane separating them inside her body. It had been so long since they'd been inside her. The doctor said she may not have an orgasm the first few times they had sex, but Calleigh felt her climax boiling low in her core, and her husbands thrust into her body over and over.

"*Gu sealladh saelbh oirnn*!"

Conor cried for heavens to preserve his sanity for his wife owned his soul. Calleigh's moans echoed in the high ceiling of their bedroom. Rick's groans rumbled beneath their bodies.

She was going to explode. The intense pleasure rippling through her body, combined with the teeming love for her husbands, overwhelmed her entire being. Her orgasm was only seconds away. She was riding that elusive crest and just needed something to send her tumbling over.

Rick slipped his fingers between his and Calleigh's bodies. His fingertip found her clit and rubbed it tiny circles. He and Conor thrust hard inside her. He felt Conor plunge deep and hold. Looking over Calleigh's shoulder, he saw his best friend's neck strain as he found release inside their wife. Calleigh's pussy clamped down as she exploded around their cocks, sending Rick over the edge into oblivion.

Long minutes later, when their breathing evened out, they separated their bodies and tucked Calleigh between them. Hands and lips crisscrossed and soothed their sensitized skin. Reaching over Rick picked up the damp cloth by their bed and tidied Calleigh then himself before handing it to Conor.

Rick turned on his side and gathered Calleigh to his front. Her head rested on the pillow beside him, and their noses rubbed. "Angel, I love you."

Conor scooted forward, so he spooned behind Calleigh. He slid the hair from the side of her neck and whispered softly in her ear, "*Is tú, mo ghrá.*"

Calleigh lay between her husbands filled with peace and joy, her love for them beyond anything she'd ever experienced. Their journey together might have started with a tragedy, but in her best friends, she became whole again. She was their love, and they were her salvation, their hearts and souls blending to form a more perfect union.

# Sneak Peak: His Perfect Partner

♥

Ethan stood, his gaze fixed on the specimen of manhood his assistant ushered into his office. Ethan imagine static electricity arcing through the air, shocking his heart back into rhythm as it stuttering against his ribs. He tried to cover his gasp by clearing his throat. A subtle, intoxicating cologne scent enhanced the recycled corporate air. Time froze, giving him ample opportunity to rake his eyes over the wet-dream-inspiring vision before him.

Dark hair swept back from the forehead of a lean face. Chiseled cheekbones and a straight nose led down to a pair of kissable lips. A strong neck disappeared into the collar of the white dress shirt. Broad shoulders filled the suit coat, which was tailored to the powerful frame. Lean hips topped long legs. Ethan's eyes drifted back up the perfect body and locked on a pair of piercing, light-colored eyes. They were a combination he'd never seen of blue and gray, and he was the target of their gaze.

He mentally slapped himself, a sharp sting jolting him back into the present, and told himself to refocus on the game. He felt arousal throb insistently behind his slacks and, concealing his excitement, offered his hand calmly.

"Ethan Harrison. It's nice to meet you."

"Special Agent Ryan Ashton."

A large, calloused hand engulfed his, the rough texture a stark contrast to his own, and he swore sparks shot out where their skin met. The strength of Special Agent Ashton's grip was undeniable, yet softened by the gentle touch of a calloused fingertip against his wrist. From long fingers, thick, bluish veins snaked across the back of the man's hand, a roadmap of vitality. The heat searing through Ethan's palm caused a shiver despite the warmth.

Ethan realized he still held Ryan's hand as he stared into those mesmerizing eyes, and he dropped his hold. He took several steps back and sat behind his desk, trying to conceal the evidence of his arousal. He pointed toward the seat opposite him, a silent invitation.

"Please sit. Make yourself comfortable. Can I get you anything to drink?"

Ryan set down his briefcase and sat in the indicated seat. He leaned back and crossed one ankle over his knee. "No, thank you."

"Special Agent Ashton, I understand you're here to hand over case information regarding the investigation of Luke Yeung and Amerisystems."

"Please call me Ryan." He picked up his briefcase. After removing a file, he placed it on the desk and leaned forward to slide it across. "You should have everything we've compiled up to this point in here."

Ethan picked the thick folder and set it to his left. He'd examine the materials later; for now, he continued talking. "Why don't you brief me on the basics while you're here?"

Ryan's relaxed posture in the chair contradicted the burn of his gaze as their eyes locked. "Our division has spent the last year compiling evidence of economic espionage against Mr. Yeung. We have documented proof of him selling the designs for Amerisystems' prototype for a new environmental monitoring device. We suspected prior leaks, yet evidence remained circumstantial."

Ethan stood and walked around his large mahogany desk to the chair next to Ryan. He sought the alluring man's closeness. He sat and mimicked the other man's posture. "What exactly does this device do?"

Ryan angled his body to better face Ethan. Their feet brushed. "It's designed to collect data on temperature, light, and soil moisture for crop lands and transfer it wirelessly to a remote computer using a short message service. This helps farmers analyze field conditions, optimizing current crop yields. In the long term, it would allow them to review the data from previous years to anticipate the condition of their fields for a new planting season."

Ethan was so caught up in watching those sensuous lips move that he almost missed his cue in the conversation. "Impressive. Who's he selling it to and why?"

Ryan shifted in his chair and licked his lips.

"He's selling it to a Chinese company which is covertly funded by the government. This company reverse engineers products from across the globe to manufacture and sell them at discounted prices. This is the first time we have evidence of them being directly supplied the design schematics. Mr. Yeung's success would significantly reduce the revenue from the release of a revolutionary device designed for and by Americans because of imitation sales."

"Well, in this economy, we can't afford for that to happen. Have you been the lead investigator?"

That little movement a moment ago had forced Ryan's jacket to separate, and Ethan caught the briefest glimpse of a thickening bulge in his lap. He was ecstatic that he wasn't the only one feeling the attraction between them.

"Yes, I have a team working with me, but I'm the point man on this one."

"Excellent. Then if I have questions, you're the one I want to speak with. Will you leave me your contact information?"

Ryan reached into his jacket pocket and removed a business card. He flipped it over, scribbled on the back, then handed it to Ethan. "Here's my card. It has all my contact information at the office."

Their hands brushed as Ryan handed off the card. A little gasp escaped as a jolt of energy made his fingers tingle. Ryan's touch lingered, then Ethan reclined as he let out a long breath. He flipped the card over and saw a series of digits. He looked over and raised one eyebrow. "And this number?"

"My personal cell phone. Just in case you need to reach me after business hours."

He smiled. He would love to connect with Ryan after business hours. Speak to, kiss, touch, fuck, be fucked ... he wasn't picky.

He glanced at his desk clock and noticed his next appointment was due in a few minutes. The half hour with Ryan had flown by. He stood and indicated for Ryan to precede him, getting a peek at Ryan's ass as he walked by. Silently, he cursed the suit coat covered it.

Ethan halted the man's progress by placing his hand on his broad shoulder and turned him around so they faced each other a foot from his office door. His hand slid down Ryan's arm a few inches, and his fingers gave a little squeeze on the hard muscle.

"It was very nice to meet you, Ryan. I will contact you if I have questions."

Ryan smiled and stepped closer until the smallest of space separated them. He tilted forward so his lips were right next to the furl of Ethan's ear. "You do that."

Ethan closed his eyes and inhaled the woodsy scent of Ryan's aftershave. The combination of Ryan's firm body nearly pressing against him and the low voice rumbling in his ear caused his cock to harden even further. He clenched his hands to prevent himself from grabbing onto the lapels of Ryan's suit coat and closing the distance between them. When he opened his eyes, Ryan had moved back and those unique blue-gray eyes held the promise of good things to come.

Ryan walked out of the Moakley court complex, into the crisp November air, and took his first solid breath in a half hour.

He dreaded the appointment beforehand. The lawyer handling the case, he'd heard, was a real ball buster. He'd never worked with the man before, but some of his colleagues had, and they said the lawyer was a nice enough guy to work with but meticulous about nailing down every minor aspect of whatever case the district attorney assigned to him. By the time Ryan left the office, his balls felt in jeopardy of busting, but only because he ached to bury himself deep inside the other man.

Ethan. The echo of his name resounded in his head.

Ryan walked to the edge of the waterfront. The smooth concrete walkway transitioned to cobblestoned bricks, smoothed by weather and time. To his right, large black rocks piled along the concrete wall and wooden beams of the old pier stuck up from the water and now acted as perches for birds scanning the harbor for their latest snack. To his left, the skyscrapers of downtown glowed in the weakening light of the late afternoon. He longed to stroll the Harborwalk, but unfinished work beckoned. He ambled his way around the building toward Northern Avenue, where he'd parked his government issued Tahoe.

Ryan climbed into the SUV. It took some creative angles and a few curses to wiggle his way out of the parking space, then headed onto Seaport Boulevard. Crossing over the bridge, he saw the Boston Tea Party ship and museum to his left. Funny, he'd lived in this city for so many years but had taken little time to explore parts of its history. He should change that. Maybe make the experience part of a date?

As he made his way through the always congested Boston traffic toward Chelsea and the FBI offices, his mind wandered back to the man he'd just left. Ethan's lean frame was only a couple of inches shorter than his own six foot five height. That would be a real bonus when he kissed the man. Those golden, hazel eyes had hypnotized him when Ethan had spoken. Ryan bet that was a real advantage in the courtroom. He wanted to sink his fingers into the thick, light brown hair on Ethan's head and wrap his arms around Ethan's trim waist. That hair was a work of art. Ryan wondered how long the man spent arranging it every morning. Was Ethan blessed with perfectly behaved hair or did he wake up looking like he stuck his finger in an electrical socket then have to tame the beast? Ryan would love to find out.

The attraction between them was undeniable. He'd seen the erection pushing against Ethan's trousers despite the man's attempt at discretion. The column had twitched as if reaching out to Ryan when he'd closed the distance between their bodies before leaving the office. Being that close had also given him the opportunity to linger in the attorney's fresh scent. Either he wasn't a user of cologne or he'd forgotten to put it on that morning because all Ryan detected was the manufactured mountain spring scent of antiperspirant and subtle hint of dry cleaning chemicals on his suit. Few could pull off a classic three piece in cobalt with pale peach tie, but Ethan *owned* that ensemble.

As he pulled into the secured lot at the office, he smiled. Wrapping up this case would be enjoyable for multiple reasons. He'd see Yeung punished; plus, he'd work with Ethan. Work closely if he got his way, which Ryan often did.

He exited the vehicle and made his way toward the front doors. Even after almost ten years in the new building, Ryan still smiled every time he walked in the door. When he'd first joined the bureau, they'd been housed in part of the Boston Government Center. The older building was tired, had antiquated facilities, and the crowded halls teemed with employees servicing multiple roles in the government. The new building was their own. Five acres and eight stories of state-of-the-art facilities provided Ryan and his colleagues room to work and support the multiple task forces needed to run the New England division of the FBI. Most of his friends thought that he only covered the greater Boston area, but in reality, his division served Maine, Massachusetts, New Hampshire, and Rhode Island. That's why Ryan frequently found himself on the road, working cases in multiple states.

He exited the elevator on the floor dedicated to white-collar crime. Not in the public eye as much as terrorism or organized crime, but his cases were not without victims. When Ryan made the switch from major crimes to white collar, his old team said he'd be bored out of his mind and begging to come back within a month. But in reality, this division forced him to use analytic and investigative skills that challenged him. He also found that since he wasn't facing the worst of society day after day, he slept better at night and didn't come home craving a drink just to wipe away the images imprinted on his brain.

"Hey Ryan, how'd it go over at the courthouse?"

"Fine. Handed over the file and the assigned attorney appeared invested in taking our guy down."

His boss, Special Agent in Charge Meier, leaned against the door frame to Ryan's office.

"Who'd you get?"

"Harrison."

"He's good. Just closed a big case with Buratti in Cyber."

"Oh yeah? On what?"

"Buratti brought him that one for the social media hacker that cyber-stalked his victims. Turns out he was also involved in cryptocurrency theft to the tune of a cool million. Harrison filed the charges three months ago and yesterday the judge sentenced the guy to five years."

"Good for them."

Meier seemed reluctant to leave his office. He kept looking around at the certificates and photos on Ryan's walls. It wasn't like his boss. Meier was a direct guy, without a lot of time for bullshit. "What's up Jeremy?"

"Listen, I've been going back and forth on whether I should say anything. Palmiotto's conviction is under review."

"What?" Ryan exclaimed.

"His attorney is filing an appeal based on the premiss that Justice Williams misapplied the state's rape shield law."

"That's bullshit!"

Meier held up his hands.

"That psycho held Svetlana prisoner for three days! She endured rape and torture. We had him dead to rights."

"Their position is that all the emails between Svetlana and Palmiotto where they talked about her sadomasochistic interests and experiences shouldn't have been excluded. Apparently, she used verbiage where she talks about being a 'pushy bottom' and enjoys being a slave to her partners. Palmiotto still says everything they did was consensual."

Ryan paced his office. Svetlana's case was the last one he worked in major crimes. The defense argued that because she engaged in the BDSM lifestyle, she asked for everything that happened to her. The lieutenant for the Manchester Police Domestic and Sexual Violence Unit in New Hampshire pulled Ryan into the case after reaching out to the FBI for help; they suspected Palmiotto wasn't a first-time offender and needed additional resources to find other potential witnesses. Ryan had worked the case for almost a year. He'd dug up three other women in two different states who'd reported crimes against Palmiotto, but the smaller police departments hadn't filed charges because of the lack of evidence. While trying the case, the U.S. Attorney masterfully argued that Svetlana's alternative lifestyle did not permit Palmiotto to hold Svetlana against her will and violate her. When they convicted and sentenced Palmiotto to twenty years, Ryan had told the division chief he needed a change. After ten years, he'd become accustomed to the stench of crime scenes and the chilling glares of remorseless criminals. But one man could only combat so much evil. He'd taken that win and seen it as a sign that his time with major crimes was ready to be sealed. Now, it threatened to unravel.

"I'll reach out to Svetlana. Does she know? If he gets a re-trial, then we need to find out if she's willing to testify again."

"She spent 20 hours on the stand last time. Both the prosecution and the defense raked that poor woman over the coals. You really think she'd volunteer to do that again?"

Ryan raked his fingers through his hair. "I don't know. Let's not worry her until we find out if a judge grants him an appeal. God, just an hour ago I thought today was one of the best I'd had in a long time, and now this."

"Yeah, sorry."

Ryan waved him off. "Not your fault. So you've worked with Harrison before?"

Meier smiled. "Yep. Great guy. Excellent attorney."

"And..."

"And what? You want me to ask him if he thinks you're cute when we're at recess next?"

"You're such an ass. I can find my own dates. Thank you very much. I just was curious if you'd ever run in the same social circles."

"I occasionally see him at professional functions, but never socially." Meier studied Ryan for a heartbeat. "You'd make a cute couple. Too bad you're Bud Light and Ethan is a delicate burgundy."

"Ouch! I can be a burgundy." Meier lifted one eyebrow. "Okay, maybe a dry cabernet. Besides, if you've never socialized with him, how do you know Ethan wouldn't like something full bodied."

"Are we still talking about wine?"

Ryan shook his head. "I don't even know. All I know is, I met this guy today, and those intense golden eyes sent a shiver down my spine. The energy between us crackled like a tesla coil, and I don't want to get my hopes up if he's taken or a pig in a designer suit."

Meier clasped Ryan's shoulder. "Every interaction I've had with him, every story I've heard, points to him being an honorable man. And you are too, Ryan. If that connection you felt is mutual, I hope you can nurture it into something deeper and more meaningful."

Once more, a vision of Ethan floated through his mind and his fingers itched to explore the body concealed by the trendy suit. Ethan's intelligence radiated from those golden eyes, and if Ryan wasn't mistaken, mischief danced in and out of the sparkles. He wanted to peel back the layers of man and find out what made up his core.

# Leave a Review

♥

Thank you so much for reading Taste of Devotion, Book Three in the Phantom River series. If you enjoyed this story, please leave a review to tell other readers how much you loved these characters. Sharing your reading experience with others on retailers and social media helps people find new reads and supports indie authors.

Thank you,

Trina Lane

# About Trina

♥

Trina is a scientist with a passion for history, music, and photography. She loves to travel and experience new places but is terminally shy around people she doesn't know. When the zombie apocalypse occurs, you'll want to find her because she's a crack shot, and promises to take out those nasty decomposing flesh-eating vermin before they have a chance to make you their snack. Her favorite aunt gave Trina a sultry romance novel to read while they were on vacation together back when Trina was in middle school and made her promise not to tell her mother. She's been hooked ever sense! Her choices in reading and writing material are as diverse as her Apple Music library, which contains music from Mozart to Metallica. Her one concession is all stories must have a happily ever after ending—did we mention she's incurably romantic? She's the mother of a very strong-willed and sweet young man who frequently makes her smile and grimace within seconds of each other. She firmly believes that the sweetness comes from her, and the other part is her husband's fault. She loves to hear from readers and her greatest wish is that we all strive to achieve bigger dreams.

# Connect with Trina

♥

- Website: www.trinalane.com

- Subscribe to my newsletter

- Email: trina@trinalane.com

- Facebook: trina.lane.books

- Facebook Group: Trina's Tantalizing Tales

- Instagram: trina.lane.books

# Other Books by Trina

♥

The Perfect Balance
The Perfect Union
His Perfect Partner
Capturing Perfection
Simply Perfection
An Imperfect Reunion
<u>Stand Alone Novels</u>
Turkish Delights
Taking the Chance
Love's Return
SEALing Fate
Paradise of Pleasure
Shield's Submissive

# About Trina

♥

Trina is a scientist with a passion for history, music, and photography. She loves to travel and experience new places but is terminally shy around people she doesn't know. When the zombie apocalypse occurs, you'll want to find her because she's a crack shot, and promises to take out those nasty decomposing flesh-eating vermin before they have a chance to make you their snack. Her favorite aunt gave Trina a sultry romance novel to read while they were on vacation together back when Trina was in middle school and made her promise not to tell her mother. She's been hooked ever sense! Her choices in reading and writing material are as diverse as her Apple Music library, which contains music from Mozart to Metallica. Her one concession is all stories must have a happily ever after ending—did we mention she's incurably romantic? She's the mother of a very strong-willed and sweet young man who frequently makes her smile and grimace within seconds of each other. She firmly believes that the sweetness comes from her, and the other part is her husband's fault. She loves to hear from readers and her greatest wish is that we all strive to achieve bigger dreams.